HANNAH AND THE HORSEMAN ON THE WESTERN TRAIL

HANNAH AND THE HORSEMAN ON THE WESTERN TRAIL

•

JOHNNY D. BOGGS

AVALON BOOKS
NEW YORK

© Copyright 1999 by Johnny D. Boggs
Library of Congress Catalog Card Number 99-90150
ISBN 0-8034-9360-6
Published by Thomas Bouregy & Co., Inc.
401 Lafayette Street, New York, NY 10003

PRINTED IN THE UNITED STATES OF AMERICA
ON ACID-FREE PAPER
BY HADDON CRAFTSMEN, BLOOMSBURG, PENNSYLVANIA

For a few influential high school teachers:
Johnny C. Moore, who liked a good western;
Jack L. Hopkins, who told a good story;
and, most importantly, Carolyn T. Newson, who taught me typing.
Happy Trails!

Chapter One

Hannah Scott screamed. Already this morning she had cut a finger slicing bacon, burned her hand on the coffeepot, and broken up a scuffle between thirteen-year-old Chris and eleven-year-old Desmond. Instead of doing chores, the two had been arguing about a baseball game they had played yesterday. On top of that, she and Pete Belissari, her boyfriend . . . fiancé . . . partner—what was he anyway?—had gotten into a fair-to-middling fight themselves after breakfast before Pete went off to look for stray cattle. And now the ever-bustling Paco had burst into the cookshed and thrust the molten shell of a tarantula into her face.

So she screamed.

It wasn't that the long-dead tarantula scared her. She didn't fear the large, furry spiders when they were

1

alive. Snakes, lizards, wolves, coyotes, and mountain lions didn't unnerve her either. You couldn't live in West Texas, more than two hundred miles from El Paso and nearly four hundred to San Antonio, and frighten easily. But she had had better days.

Paco yelled himself, dropped the dead spider, and darted out of the building, leaving the door wide open. Hannah recovered and kicked the tarantula's remains outside. She took a deep breath and ran her fingers, ignoring the flour on them, through her blond hair. She was twenty-seven now, but felt a lot older. Pete said she spread herself too thin, and he was probably right. She oversaw an orphanage, caring for seven youths between eight and thirteen years old, and a ranch, and up until two months ago she had been a partner in a stagecoach line from Fort Stockton to Presidio.

Stage line president Dean Everhart had bought out her interest. Pete and good friend Buddy Pecos begrudgingly also sold out to Everhart. The stagecoaches kept coming through for about a month. Then Everhart lost the Argo Stagecoach Company in a high-stakes poker game in Shafter, the winner sold off the assets and headed to Tombstone, and Everhart, disheartened, moved back to Memphis to tend to his sick mother. Or as Buddy Pecos said, ''He lit a shuck for Tennessee to live off his po' mama.''

Hannah walked to the main yard. She stared briefly at a cloudless sky and turned toward Limpia Creek just across the road that wound down Wild Rose Pass and to Fort Davis, ten miles south. Spring ushered in the first rainy season in the Big Bend region, but this year the rains hadn't come and only dust flowed over the rocks in the creek bed. Spring was also supposed to be mild, but the sun scorched the Davis Mountains and surrounding valleys. If March was this hot, Hannah dreaded June.

In front of the barn, the children played another game of baseball. Their dog lounged on the porch, her tail thumping on the wood, as if interested in the game. Hannah forced a smile as ten-year-old Cynthia hit the ball over Desmond's head and took off running.

"No! No! No!" Chris screamed as Desmond and his twin sister, Darcy, chased after the ball as it rolled toward the well. "Run to first base! Not third base! You're running the wrong way! Cynthia!"

At least the children could enjoy life, Hannah thought. They didn't have to worry about things like loan payments and cattle dying of thirst, and heated exchanges with a boyfriend-fiancé-partner. Hannah had taken her profits from the Argo Stagecoach sale and, after buying the children clothes and books, bought a herd of cattle and an adjoining section of land. She had to borrow money from the Fort Davis Bank to complete the transaction, but the banker was more than willing to lend her the cash—this was cattle country, after all—providing Pete Belissari and Buddy Pecos cosigned the note.

That had brought on a debate-turned-argument between Hannah and Pete. "I'm no cattleman, Hannah," Pete had said. "I'm a horseman, a mustanger."

"Buddy knows cattle. And you can learn."

Pecos shrugged. Pete shook his head.

"Listen," Hannah said, feeling her face flush. "We don't have the stagecoach to bring in money anymore, and I've got seven children to feed. This ranch is mine, but I'm offering you a partnership in it. Unless you can think of a better way to make a living out here."

This ranch is mine. She regretted those words now. It had been almost two years ago that Pete arrived at her front door. She would have lost the ranch then if not for him, and Buddy. And the two had saved her life countless times since; of course, she had saved their hides a time or two. But still . . . they had as much right to this land as she did.

They signed the agreement, though. Reluctantly, maybe, but they signed. But now Hannah wondered if Pete had been right. He was smarter than she was about *some* things; Hannah could admit that. He had graduated from the University of Louisville, and she had struggled to get out of an Austin orphanage. What was it Pete had said? "This country is full of cheap grass and people who are cow poor. You sure that's what you want?"

Hannah wasn't sure now. She only wished Pete would be a little more supportive about working cattle.

She smelled something burning. Hannah turned and walked behind the cabin. Smoke poured from the doorway to the cookshed. With an unladylike ranch-yard expletive, she ran inside and slapped the burning skillet with her apron. Yes, it was going to be a rotten day, and 1886 was shaping up to be one miserable year.

The claybank gelding was green and skittish, which was why Pete Belissari saddled it that morning. Dardanus needed the work, and if Pete had to spend all day looking after stupid cows he could at least get some pleasure by training a cow pony.

Belissari loved working with horses. He had spent years in West Texas chasing down wild mustangs, breaking them, and selling them to the Army or ranches before the Army business dried up and the horse herds practically disappeared. One thing he had appreciated about the stagecoach business was working with horses that weren't saddle mounts: German Oldenburgs and big Americans that pulled stagecoaches. That had been a new experience, and he enjoyed the challenge.

Working cattle was new, too, even a challenge—but he wouldn't call eating dust and chasing the big mossy horns out of thickets enjoyable. Maybe he could tolerate it more if he and Hannah quit sniping at each other. He had met her in May of '84, and after a whirlwind courtship, they were supposed to have been married. But the wedding, because of some violent happenings beyond their control, had been postponed. They hadn't even talked about marriage for almost a year now. Their relationship had been on a plateau, and now it felt as if they were about to push each other off a mesa.

He was furious at Hannah, furious at himself, for being talked into this cattle operation. He enjoyed a good beefsteak as much as anyone in these parts, but as a Greek, his favorite food remained his mother's *fasola'tha,* the bean soup she always served during Lent. Maybe it wasn't that he hated cattle; he just didn't want to be a cowboy. Pete Belissari was a horseman, plain and simple.

Still, he reined in Dardanus when he spotted the brown form below. The longhorn cow lay on her side beside a small grove of juniper at the bottom of the hill. The hillside wasn't that steep, but small volcanic rocks and loose shale lined the path down. Pete wasn't so sure he wanted to test the claybank on a tricky way down a rocky slope, but he didn't want to half-walk, half-slide his way down in his worn-out moccasins either. Nor did he want to leave Dardanus ground-reined up here while he checked out the cow below.

"I should have saddled Poseidon," he said to himself, tugging the reins with his right hand and giving the gelding a quick kick in the ribs. The claybank turned, snorted, hesitating as Pete sucked in fresh air and held his breath. Another kick and Dardanus cautiously stuck its right forefoot on the slope. Belissari leaned back in the saddle, expelled his lungs, and gave the gelding some encouragement.

They worked well together, picking a cautious path to solid footing at the base of the hill. Pete leaned forward and patted the claybank's neck and headed toward the longhorn. He didn't get far before Dardanus stutter-stepped and balked.

"Easy," Belissari said, and frowned. The smell hit him then, making him want to spit. He jerked the reins, kicked the claybank hard, and made a wide arc around the junipers before dismounting upwind of the longhorn. After wrapping the reins around a small boulder, he fished a knife from the saddlebags. "Stay here," he told the gelding and pulled the red cotton bandanna over his nose as he approached the junipers and the dead cow.

Seven junipers grew here in a cavelike semicircle. The longhorn had collapsed—from a lack of thirst, Pete guessed—and tried to crawl to the shade but made it only halfway to the opening. She was already starting to bloat, but the wolves and turkey vultures hadn't gotten to her yet, so he could salvage her hide. The tannery in El Paso would pay a few dollars for a cowhide. That was far from the thirty or better a longhorn would fetch at the Kansas cowtowns, but it was something. Enough to buy some beers, whiskey, and a cigar at Lightner's Saloon in Fort Davis to kill the bitter taste in his mouth.

He knelt, gagging as he began working with the razor-sharp skinning knife. Sharp rocks bit through his gray trousers—*Should have worn chaps,* he thought—and blood stained the sleeves of the blue calico shirt he had paid fifty cents for just last week at the Robbins & Todd mercantile in town. He took off his battered tan hat and rested it on a juniper branch and brushed back his long brown hair, forgetting about the blood and grime that stained his fingers.

Buddy Pecos could skin a dead cow in minutes; it would take Pete half a day. He grabbed his hat, shook his head, and backed away from the junipers, ripping down the bandanna as he hunched over. Bracing his hands over his knees, he breathed deeply, quickly, searching, desperately for air that didn't smell like decaying flesh. Dardanus suddenly whinnied and pawed the ground furiously. Belissari looked up just in time to see the claybank rear, breaking its tether, turn, and gallop away.

A heavy snort sounded behind him. Pete slowly donned his hat, took a step back, and looked around at the mulberry-colored longhorn bull fifteen yards from him. Pete knew El Moro on sight—he had slapped the SBP Connected brand on the wild-eyed, seventeen-hundred-pound man-hater's flank himself. El Moro lost his left eye in a fight with a mountain lion in January, but the cougar got the worst end of the bull's heavy, curved horns that spread more than seven feet. Mucus leaked from El Moro's nostrils like beer from a tapped keg at Lightner's on Saturday night. The bull lowered his massive head and began pawing the ground, sending thick dust skyward.

Pete dropped the useless skinning knife and ran. He leaped over the bloody carcass of the dead longhorn and into the small clearing between the junipers. His right hand grasped a limb on a half-dead tree and he pulled himself up as El Moro roared and charged.

Belissari had left his revolver holstered on his nightstand back at the ranch, and his Winchester was sheathed in the saddle scabbard on Dardanus, who by now was probably halfway to Mexico. El Moro stopped by the dead longhorn, sniffed for a minute, and backed away, his one good eye on Pete.

The longhorn turned and circled the junipers. For a minute, Pete thought the bull would leave, but then he knew El Moro was only looking for another way to attack him—and it didn't take the beast long to find a weak spot. The back of the junipers faced open country, giving the bull a clear shot at the sickly, sixteen-foot-high tree Pete had perched himself on. El Moro snorted and attacked. Belissari scrambled as high as he could go before the bull slammed into the tree. The juniper shook and creaked as bark flew, and Pete clenched both fists around two twisted limbs and braced his feet in a knotty fork just inches out of El Moro's reach.

El Moro backed away. Pete looked up and saw dust on the hilltop. The bull shook his head and pawed the earth again. A rider appeared on a dun horse, too far away to make out. Belissari didn't care, didn't even think about pride. He lifted his hat and waved it in the air, shouting for help and praying that the traveler would see or hear him.

El Moro's hooves pounded again. The bull slammed into the tree again, harder this time, snapping off a lower limb and tilting the tree back several degrees as roots popped out of the dry soil nearby. Pete lost his footing but held onto the limbs and quickly pulled himself up. The blow knocked the bull to his knees and left a thin cut on his head. El Moro was slow getting up, leaving a trail of mucus and blood as he hobbled away and turned to face the juniper once more.

Belissari pulled off his hat and waved frantically. ''Thank you, Apollo,'' he said as the rider slowed, turned, and headed down the hillside, pulling a rifle from the saddle scabbard. Belissari had to admire the man's horsemanship. The bull glanced at the newcomer, shook his head, and snorted again, then trotted away as the rider neared.

Pete let out a heavy sigh and dropped from the tree, watching, making sure El Moro was gone. Satisfied, he pulled the hat down on his head and turned at the sound of trotting hooves. His smile was short-lived. Belissari immediately recognized the man on the dun horse.

''I should have taken my chances with the bull,'' he said aloud.

Chapter Two

"**Y**es sir, this is a sad, sad situation," the rider said, sweeping off a shapeless slouch hat and wiping sweat off his brow. "I knew the mustang business had played out in these parts, but I never thought I'd live to see the great Petros Belissari forced to start straddling trees."

He was a black man, with a back so straight he seemed to be standing at attention while sitting in one of those uncomfortable Army-issue McClellan saddles. He sported a couple weeks' growth of stubble on his face, and gray now dominated his close-cropped hair. The saddle, Springfield rifle, and hat were regulation U. S. Cavalry, but the Apache-style moccasins, just like Belissari's, pillow-ticking shirt, canvas trousers, and black vest were anything but military.

"And you're a long way from Arizona Territory, Sergeant Major Cadwallader," Belissari said, "and out of uniform to boot."

Robert Cadwallader's head snapped up. "I am in the proper uniform, sir, of a retired noncommissioned officer on his way home." The all-Army, ex–buffalo soldier pulled on his hat, dropped from the saddle, and extended a leathery hand that Pete quickly accepted.

"Good to see you, mister," Cadwallader said.

Belissari nodded at the dust from El Moro's retreat. "Better to see you, Sergeant Major . . . for once."

Pete had dealt with Cadwallader for a few years when the Tenth Cavalry was stationed at Fort Davis. With the end of the Indian Wars in Texas, Colonel Benjamin H. Grierson's old regiment had been transferred west to Whipple Barracks last April to help subdue the Apache. The last Belissari heard, Cadwallader was stationed at Fort Thomas while General Crook and the Third Cavalry were hunting down Geronimo south of the border.

"Retired?" Pete said questioningly.

"I'm getting a little long in the tooth to be chasing Apache. Soldiering is a young man's game, Mr. Belissari. Do you know Beto Mendietta?"

Pete nodded. He had traded horses with Beto many a time. The ancient Mexican's ranch was just off the San Antonio–El Paso Road northeast of town and neighbored the Spring Valley spread Colonel Grierson bought back in '84. Mendietta got most of his water from Limpia Creek. He was hurting just like all of the Davis Mountain ranches.

"Cowboying?" Belissari's eyes twinkled.

Cadwallader cleared his throat. "Ranching," he corrected.

Pete chuckled and started to say something else, but the sergeant cut him off. "Mr. Belissari," he said, "I would enjoy chatting with you and hearing all about how you came to saddle that juniper, but, sir, this place stinks to high heaven."

Cadwallader helped Belissari finish skinning the longhorn, and the two rode double toward the Wild Rose Ranch Pete called home. Pete had been lucky that the old Army veteran happened along, and his good fortune held. They found Dardanus a couple miles away, chewing on grama grass. Pete dropped from the dun's back and eased his way to the gelding. More good luck: The temperamental claybank didn't spook when Belissari reached for the reins. Belissari tightened the cinch and swung into the saddle, letting out a sigh of relief and an *efhi'* for his deliverance.

At least now he wouldn't have to return to the ranch, in front of Hannah and the kids, bouncing on the back of Cadwallader's dun with his arms around the sergeant major's waist.

Hannah smiled when Sergeant Major Cadwallader wrapped his reins around the near post of the main corral. She had known few enlisted men, but had always been fond of the tall soldier who kept his uniform free of dust while on the post—and that took some doing in a place like Fort Davis. The stories, tall tales perhaps, in town claimed that Cadwallader had been a free man in Chicago, working in the slaughterhouses, before joining the Union Army during the late War for another kind of slaughter. They say he survived the massacre at Fort Pillow in Tennessee and was considered the top soldier in the Eleventh U.S. Colored Troops. After the War, he joined Ben Grierson's Tenth Cavalry and quickly became that regiment's top soldier. Grierson himself had personally recommended the soldier for the Medal of Honor for his actions against Victorio's Apache forces in 1879. Cadwallader was still the talk of the garrison and the town despite the fact that the Tenth had been gone for almost a year. But she was surprised when Cadwallader told her he had retired. The man had known nothing but Army for more than twenty years.

"Captain Kaye resigned, the colonel retired, even old Captain Leslie has called it quits. This man's army just wasn't this man's army anymore," Cadwallader said, jerking a thumb toward his chest.

"Well, you're welcome here. We can use a good hand."

"Thank you, Miss Scott, but I'm partnering with Beto Mendietta. In fact, I should be on my way."

"You'll do no such thing, Serg . . . Mr. Cadwallader. At least until you've had some coffee and biscuits. That should tide you over till you reach *Señor* Beto's. He'll be coming over here tomorrow for a rancher's meeting. Will you?"

"I don't know, ma'am. That's the first I've heard of this meeting."

"Me too," Belissari said.

Hannah turned and studied Pete briefly. His hands were brown and grimy, shirtsleeves filthy, and he looked a little pale for having been out in the sun all day. He was right; cowboying didn't agree with him.

"Pete, honey," she said, a touch of sarcasm in her voice, "you said yourself that you'd rather concentrate on the horse business and Buddy and I could handle the cattle end."

"He might need some help with those horses, Miss Scott," Cadwallader said. "Why, when I came across him, he was trying to ride a dried-up juniper to a standstill."

Hannah looked back at the visitor. His dark eyes glinted like diamonds. She glanced at Pete. His face began to flush, and there was no amusement dancing in his eyes as he stared at Cadwallader. She mumbled an "I see" and smiled at the old soldier.

"Sunstroke," Cadwallader said. "That's my guess. Maybe there's some Greek myth about a tree turning into a unicorn."

"No," Pete said, finally grinning, "but Zeus once chained Prometheus to a mountain and tortured him . . . which is what I should have done to you."

Buddy Pecos had to stoop to get through the cabin's doorway. Hannah poured him a cup of coffee as he pulled up a chair next to Pete at the table. The ranch foreman, Pecos was the most imposing man she had ever known. He was built like a telegraph pole, six-foot-five, leathery and hard-muscled, with a scarred face, mangled ear, and brown leather patch over his right eye. His sandy brown hair was thin, streaked with gray, and a high-crowned black Stetson with a five-inch brim topped his head. He didn't remove the hat. At least Pete took off his hat when indoors, but Hannah accepted Buddy Pecos—bad manners and all.

"Talk in Shafter is that Milton Faver's roundin' up cattle with the neighborin' ranches and plannin' a drive to Kansas," Pecos said to no one in particular.

"I'm sure that's why Julian Cale has called an association meeting for here tomorrow," Hannah said. "You'll be here, won't you, Buddy?"

Cale owned the biggest spread near Fort Davis and had founded the Limpia Creek Cattleman's Association. Hannah didn't care much for the name—Cattle-*man's*—but she was a member nonetheless. She'd have a busy day tomorrow, cooking biscuits and making coffee for all of her neighbors as they discussed their options and complained about the drought.

"No, ma'am," Pecos replied. "I found a couple more beeves dead. That's seven we've lost this month."

"Eight," Pete said. "I found one this morning."

Hannah felt weak. Inside she cursed the weather. When she first arrived in West Texas, she found it amusing how the ranchers, farmers, and sheepherders always looked at the sky, searching for clouds, silently praying for rain. Now she did the same thing. She had lost more than a dozen head this year, and summer was a long way off.

"Anyway," Pecos continued, "I was hopin' I could borrow young Chris and drive a few head down the pass to this li'l water hole I found before it dries up."

"Chris?"

"Got the makin's of a good cowboy, ma'am."

"He'll be disappointed," Hannah said. "I think Mr. Cale is bringing his nephew over."

Chris met Paul Richmond at the Presbyterian Church two months ago, and they quickly became good friends. They were the same age, enjoyed horses and baseball, and both were orphans. Chris had never known his parents. All that Hannah had been told was that Chris's mother had worked at The Cribs in the part of Fort Davis known as Chihuahua, the part of town decent folks avoided. She had died of consumption when Chris was an infant. And his father? Who knew? Paul's parents had drowned in a flash flood around Llano shortly after Christmas, and the boy had been sent to live with his uncle.

"I think Chris would prefer cowboyin'," Pecos said. "Give him something to brag about. And Pete's gonna be needed here, gettin' some horses ready to work longhorns."

Pete placed his coffee cup in front of his empty plate. "You think Cale will want to drive a herd to Kansas?"

"Most likely. We got too many cattle grazin',

drought ain't shown no signs of lettin' up. Best remedy
I know is to get the cattle off the land. Best way to do
that is head 'em north. And we'll have to provide Cale
with some help. Horses, I expect.'' He smiled at Belissari. ''That's your job, pard.''

Belissari smoothed his mustache. ''How many
horses are we looking at?''

Pecos sipped coffee and slid back as Hannah ladled
stew onto his plate. He thanked her, scratched his chin,
and considered Pete's question for a minute. He
spooned a healthy helping of stew and shoveled the
food into his mouth, finally answering while chewing.

''Well . . . figure on two thousand . . . twenty-five
hundred head . . . 'bout a dozen waddies . . . I'd say . . .
six mounts apiece . . . What's that? Sixty?''

''Seventy-two.''

Buddy swallowed and refilled his mouth. ''Need
more . . . just to . . . round them dogies up. Now . . .
Mr. Cale . . .''

Hannah refilled both men's cups, stopping long
enough to glare at Pecos. Leaving his hat on was one
thing, but this . . . Buddy got the message. He swallowed, wiped his mouth with the back of his hand, and
apologized.

''Anyway,'' he continued, ''Mr. Cale will provide
most of the horses. My guess is he'll want you to break
'em while everyone else pitches in to help with the
roundup.''

Hannah cleared her throat. ''You think that's the
best way, Buddy? A cattle drive?''

Buddy shrugged. ''Cale will offer you a fair price so the risk is on him to get them longhorns to market. Lest you wanna drive 'em to Dodge City your ownself.'' The tall man's lone blue eye twinkled, and Hannah smiled at him.

But her mind raced as she washed the dishes after Pecos and Pete retired for the evening. Julian Cale was a good man, a friend, a knowledgeable rancher who had been up the cattle trails before. Buddy Pecos had driven cattle himself up the Shawnee and Chisholm trails before they closed. Pete knew horses better than anyone she had ever met.

She ran her wet fingers over her dry lips, her thoughts again on Julian Cale. He could be a regular skinflint at times. Buddy said Cale would offer a ''fair'' price for their cattle, but Hannah doubted if she and the miserly rancher would ever agree on just what constituted ''fair.'' Besides, Hannah didn't want a *fair* price; she wanted a *great* one.

She checked on the children and stepped outside, sitting on an oak keg on the porch and scratching the collie's ears. The dog wagged her tail appreciatively. Somewhere past Wild Rose Pass, a wolf howled, and the horses stirred uncomfortably in the corrals. The night was cool, a welcome change from the unseasonably hot days, but the wind blew dust across the yard.

Buddy Pecos was right. They had to do something, or all of the cattle would soon die. She would listen to what Julian Cale had to say tomorrow, but she'd also listen to her gut.

Chapter Three

It seemed as if half of Presidio County had descended on Wild Rose Ranch that morning. The meeting was supposed to be for the Limpia Creek Cattleman's Association, but almost every rancher had brought his entire family. Hannah hadn't worked this hard since feeding passengers back when the Argo Stagecoach Company was in business. Children dashed about in the yard, women gossiped underneath the patio built for the stage line's passengers and workers, and cowboys and cattlemen idled about the corral, barn, and lean-to, waiting to get down to business—once Julian Cale showed up.

Hannah again walked to the well. These men drank coffee like water. As she rested by the limestone structure, her blue eyes searched the smaller corral near the barn where a crowd of cowboys had gathered around to watch Pete work that jittery claybank, Dardanus.

Pete slung a saddle over a fence rail, stepped out of the corral, and shook hands with a Mexican who had just dismounted a muscular dapple mare. Dardanus trotted around the corral nervously while most of the cowboys began rolling cigarettes or working giant wads of chewing tobacco into their cheeks. *Buddy says Chris will make a fine cowboy. I hope the boy doesn't pick up their bad habits.* She shook her head and listened as Pete and the Mexican talked.

"Buenos días, mi amigo," the old man told Pete. *"¿Cómo está usted?"*

"Kalime'ra ke kalo's i'rthate," Pete replied. *"Koura'stika."* His head jerked toward the gelding.

Out here, it was common for a Mexican to ask a question in Spanish and an American to answer in English. This close to the border, people were often bilingual but felt more comfortable speaking their own language. Pete and Beto Mendietta had a private joke, however. Beto spoke in Spanish; Pete replied in Greek—but only in greetings. Pete was probably the only Texan west of the Brazos who read and wrote Greek.

"¿Dónde está Señor Cale?"

"He's late," Pete replied in English. "But Hannah has some coffee and biscuits ready."

"Gracias."

Hannah smiled. Occasional problems with the language barrier remained, and one involved Julian Cale

and Mendietta's son, Faustino. Last fall, Cale had hired
the young Mexican to paint a barn. The rancher didn't
have enough red or white paint to do the entire job
(and was too tight to buy more) so he told Faustino to
mix the paint together, figuring that a lighter shade of
red would do the job well enough. When Cale returned
to inspect his barn, he saw—to his chagrin—the building painted red and white like a Christmas peppermint
stick. He paid Faustino anyway, didn't repaint the barn,
and never said a word to the Mexican's father. Julian
Cale respected the elder Mendietta too much.

Once, the old vaquero had been one of *los Kineños,*
the riders who worked for Richard King's great ranch
between Corpus Christi—Pete's birthplace—and
Brownsville. But Beto Mendietta did something few of
the King's Men ever did: He left.

After saving his wages for almost twenty years, he
got a job with the Texas and New Orleans Railroad
and worked his way west before buying his own small
spread near Fort Davis.

Years in the sun had baked his wrinkled face and
bony hands a deep brown, which made his black eyes
and short white beard stand out. He wore a flat-
crowned chocolate hat, old brogans, blue flannel shirt,
and Mexican denim jeans held up by a pair of frayed
suspenders. In his left hand he held a wooden cane,
which he needed to walk these days. Of course, Beto
seldom walked anywhere. He'd ride twenty yards
rather than cross a street.

Which is what he did now. The old-timer mounted

his dapple mare and trotted across the yard to the main cabin, tipping his hat and bowing slightly as he passed Hannah and saying, *"La Patrona, muchas gracias por la invitación."*

"You are quite welcome, *Señor* Mendietta," she said and turned her attention toward the four riders riding down the brown, rugged peak east of the ranch.

Dardanus was in a stubborn mood this morning, showing off for the spectators. Pete held a bridle in his left hand, but the gelding had no intention of being caught this morning. Every time Belissari came close to cornering the claybank, Dardanus bolted to the other side of the corral—much to the delight of the area waddies.

"That's showin' him who's boss!" one cowboy yelled.

"You're one *muy bueno caballero*, Belissari!" another chimed in.

Pete just smiled, spread his arms and slowly approached the gelding, talking softly, easily, trying to befriend the gelding. Belissari knew what he was doing. He had seen cowboys who would beat a stubborn, green mount senseless, break the animal's spirit to show who's the leader. That wasn't Belissari's way; he didn't even wear spurs.

"Come on, boy," he whispered. "We've done this before."

Dardanus's nostrils flared. Pete stopped and waited for the horse to relax. The gelding lifted its head and snorted. Belissari took another step. Closer. Closer. He frowned as the gelding whinnied and bolted just out of his grasp.

Shaking his head but still smiling, he turned around. The smile vanish when he saw a lariat sail over the claybank's head. The rope tightened and nearly jerked the gelding off his feet.

"Here you go, pard," a grinning cowboy said as he slid off a sorrel quarter horse. "All ready to be rode now."

Belissari walked to Dardanus, removed the hemp rope, and attached the bridle, then led the claybank to the edge of the corral where the saddle and still-smiling cowhand awaited.

The cowboy had the curliest brown hair Pete had seen, and wore a gray Stetson at a rakish angle. His brown Coffeyville boots shined like his saddle, and he wore fire-blued spurs with jingle bobs and an overlaid nickel star that must have set him back a month's pay.

"Looks like you needed a hand." Pete liked the cadence of most Texas cowboys, but this waddie's twang frayed his nerves.

"The idea," Belissari said deliberately, "was so the horse wouldn't become scared of a rope."

The cowboy's smile disappeared. He carefully began coiling his lariat. "Looked like you'd spend all spring runnin' that fellow down. Anyway, I just hate to see a man a-foot." He secured the lariat to his saddle horn and led his sorrel to the other corral.

"I see you've met my new foreman," Julian Cale said.

Belissari's eyes followed the cowboy. Hannah and Cale's nephew, Paul, carried a bucket from the well to the cabin. Pete wondered if she had witnessed the incident. Then he noticed Irwin Sawyer watering three horses. Cale had just arrived, bringing his nephew and two hired hands with him. Sawyer was a young, ignorant cowhand who worked for Cale and harbored strong feelings for Hannah. Pete didn't like Sawyer. His eyes fell again on Cale's new foreman. It seemed the rancher made a habit of hiring cowboys Pete Belissari didn't like, and Pete liked most people.

"Times are hard, I guess," Pete said, shaking Cale's hand.

For once, the rancher's cold eyes danced with amusement. A heavy man with a bum shoulder that rendered his left arm useless, he favored his leg because of a mangled foot. Both injuries were the results of bullet wounds suffered while helping Hannah.

"Pete, Cal Maddox is a top hand. Don't you go get no notions about whipping the tar out of him just yet. I'll need him on the trail to Dodge."

Belissari forgot about the quick-roping waddie and Dardanus for the moment. "You're taking a herd to Kansas?"

Cale nodded. "I am; we'll see what these other association members want. And I figure I might could hire you to ride the rough off my remuda before we hit the trail. Give you a fair price."

Fair? Pete thought. *Not without a lot of haggling.* Still, his dark eyes twinkled and he jerked a thumb toward Maddox. "Now, Julian," he said, his voice brimming with sarcasm, "if you've hired yourself such a top hand, why don't you let him break your horses?"

" 'Cause I like the job done right the first time."

Pete grinned. Cale quickly added, "And I'll need Cal rounding up the horses. Good cowboys are hard to come by. A bronc-buster, a horseman or mustanger . . . them guy's are cheaper than bad whiskey."

Cale's laugh boomed in the morning, and several of the other cowboys joined in. Belissari shook his head, laughing at himself as he headed back into the corral to work Dardanus. The old rancher had set him up . . . again.

He gingerly entered the cabin with his left hand pressed against his aching back. The children were already asleep, and Pete had missed supper while shoeing the horses and giving his favorite mounts, Poseidon, Duck Pegasus, and Lightning Flash, extra grooming. He poured himself a cup of coffee and stared at Hannah.

She sat at the kitchen table, chewing on a pencil and staring at the chicken-scratch notes in front of her. The coal-oil lantern cast a warm glow on her face. She is, Pete thought, quite beautiful. He hated to interrupt her thoughts. He could stare at her like this for hours.

"How did the meeting go?" he finally asked. He had been out with Dardanus when the meeting broke up and hadn't seen Hannah since that morning.

"Chris and Buddy didn't come back," she said softly, not answering the question.

"Probably made camp in the hills. Moving cows takes time."

She nodded, placed the pencil on the table and rubbed her temples.

"The meeting?" Pete prompted.

"Mr. Cale is heading a drive to Dodge City," she answered. "He'll buy any cattle we want to send with him for fifteen dollars a head."

Belissari nodded. "That's better than they'll fetch down here."

"And half what they're worth in Kansas." Her voice had an edge to it now.

No more arguments, Pete said to himself and moved to the table, pulling up a chair opposite her and settling in with a groan.

"We can't very well drive our herd to Kansas, Hannah," he said.

"We can go with Mr. Cale," she said.

Pete's mouth dropped. "Huh?"

"Here's the deal accepted by the association. Mr. Cale will buy any association member's cattle for fifteen a head. Or, each member will provide four workers for the drive and take full profits of their cattle less two dollars a head to cover expenses."

Tugging the ends of his mustache, Belissari ran the proposition and Hannah's explanation through his mind twice. Hannah would have to send four cowboys up the drive with Julian's men. She had one experienced drover: Buddy Pecos.

"Hannah," he said, "the onus is on Julian to get

the herd to Kansas. If he pays you fifteen a head, it doesn't matter if the entire herd drowns in the Red River, your money's in the bank. But if you send four cowhands up the trail—four cowhands we don't have— and something happens to the herd, you lose everything.''

''I'm willing to take that gamble.''

''What if there's a glut in Kansas? What if they bring only ten dollars a head?''

''They won't. You know that.''

He breathed deeply, exhaled, and took another sip of coffee. Pete had seen that look in Hannah's eyes before. Stubborn. He decided on another approach.

''Where are you going to find four cowboys?''

''Buddy,'' she said. ''And you.''

''Me?'' He laughed aloud. ''Hannah, I'm no cow-hand. I've never been on a trail drive.''

''But you know horses. And Mr. Cale will need a wrangler to handle the remuda. He even suggested you at the meeting.''

Silence fell upon the small room. The knot tighten-ing in Belissari's stomach didn't come from hunger. ''That's two.''

''I have to go.''

''Not a chance.''

She stood up, her eyes fuming. ''Don't tell me 'not a chance,' Pete! That's part of the deal. If an associa-tion member elects to accompany the drive, the owner has to go.''

She turned around to make sure her outburst hadn't

wakened the children. "The only reason Julian said that was to keep you from going," Pete said. "He knows just how mule-headed you can be."

"He doesn't know me well enough, then," she snapped, though she kept her voice down this time. "You're right. I can't drive a herd, but I can handle a team, and he'll need someone to drive a hoodlum wagon."

Belissari shook his head. The hoodlum wagon carried bedrolls and tack, and the driver might help the chuckwagon cook. Sometimes, the hoodlum driver also served as a nighthawk, watching the remuda at night. Hannah wouldn't be able to do that—well, she could, but Cale would never permit it—but she could drive the wagon.

"Julian won't allow it."

"He doesn't have any choice. That's part of the association's agreement. He won't like it, but he'll do it."

Pete felt defeated. It wasn't the first time. He seldom won arguments with Hannah.

"What about the kids?"

Now she smiled. "You didn't see Mrs. Appletree this morning, did you?" Belissari's head had barely started to shake before Hannah continued. "Well, she and Mr. Appletree brought along Joshua Lake to the meeting. Mr. Lake is the new schoolteacher in town, and Betty wanted him to meet me. It also turns out that he'll need a place to rent, and after the meeting, I started thinking and got to talking to him and he agreed to stay here while we're gone and watch after the children. And having a real, honest-to-goodness school-teacher would be a world of good for all of the children, Darcy and Desmond especially.'' She smiled. ''And I asked Mr. Lake if he enjoys Homer. He loves *The Odyssey* and can't wait to meet you.''

Pete couldn't help himself. He laughed. Hannah moved closer, sat on the edge of the table, and placed her slender fingers on his aching shoulders.

''You're a pretty amazing businesswoman, Miss Scott,'' Pete said.

''Pete, let's not fight. Not about this. You'll go, won't you? We could pretend it's a vacation.''

''Vacation? A dozen or more rapacious waddies and—yeah, I'll go. You know that.''

She bent forward and kissed his forehead. ''I worked through the math all day, Pete,'' she said. ''Yes, it's a gamble. But selling out for fifteen a head barely gets us through the winter with the bank note due and all. It just makes more sense to go to Kansas, maybe double our profits.''

Belissari's smile faded. He did his own math: Hannah and Buddy and him totaled three. ''Who's the fourth?''

She sighed. ''We'll have to hire someone,'' she said.

''No you won't,'' a voice answered. ''I'm going.''

Both turned. In the doorway stood Chris.

Chapter Four

He slammed into the ground, sliding and spinning as pebbles tore into his cheek and the air exploded from his lungs. Pete landed faceup, trying to remember how to breathe, then quickly rolled underneath the corral's lowest rail as the fourteen-hand flea-bitten gray gelding charged.

Someone handed him two canteens. He blinked. No, there was only one. He took it and swished the iron-tasting liquid around in his mouth and spit out blood and dirt. When his breathing finally relaxed, he wiped the pebbles off his face, at least those not embedded deep in his cheek.

"Vacation," he said dryly.

"¿Como?"

Pete lifted his head to see Faustino Mendietta, looking far from a vaquero in his dingy cotton clothes, wooden sandals, and gray derby with a turkey feather in its band. Belissari took another swing of water, corked the canteen, and handed it back to his bronc-busting helper.

"Nothing," he said. "A joke." The teenager stared at him blankly. *"Broma."*

Faustino grinned. *"Ah, chistoso, sí,"* he said, then fired off something in Spanish way too fast for Pete to comprehend. Slowly the horseman pulled himself to his feet, let out something that was part-sigh, part-groan, and turned to face the gray bronc. A dollar a horse was all Julian Cale would fork over—"I pay my cowboys a dollar a day, and that's more than most of them are worth," the rancher argued. "I sure ain't about to give you more than a buck a bronc to gentle them nags!"— and it seemed that Cale had filled his remuda with every widow-maker, every buzzard-head, every cribber and ridge runner west of the Pecos.

"Thé mou!" Pete said with a growl. "The whole lot's not worth a gallon of glue."

He picked up his hat, slapped it against his aching leg, grabbed his lariat, shook out a loop, and moved closer to the gray raw one that snorted defiantly and bolted as Pete let the rope sail.

The hemp lariat burned through his vest as he gritted his teeth and fought his way to the center post in Cale's corral. Faustino also lassoed the gelding with a perfect toss, and the two managed to pull the horse up tight through a chocking dust kicked up by the rearing, turning horse. Once Pete wrapped his lariat around the post, the Mexican lad tossed a blanket over the bronc's head. The gray, which Pete had named Crockhead, relaxed, but his body trembled as Faustino tightened the cinch on the bronc saddle.

Belissari patted Crockhead's neck and sang softly as he gripped the hackamore and cautiously removed the two lariats. The gray's eyes opened wide. Pete motioned Faustino away with his left hand, then bit Crockhead's ear and swung into the saddle, pulling back the hackamore and digging his knees into the gelding's sides as the bronc reared and twisted.

The horse's quick, wild moves jarred every bone in Pete's body. Belissari's hat flew into the wind and for a moment he thought his breakfast would follow. His teeth slammed together so hard a spasm of pain shot through his head. Crockhead bolted to the edge of the corral and tried to leave Belissari's body in a bloody heap on the cedar posts, then lowered his head and sent his rear legs high. Pete lost his balance and decided it was time to skedaddle, so he released the hackamore and bailed off the rank bronc. He landed easier this time only to trip over his own hat and taste gravel again.

He hoped young Chris was having as much fun at the roundup.

The boy had won the argument with Hannah. Belissari knew he would. The teen could be as mule-headed as Hannah, and he put up a good fight. Julian Cale was sending his own nephew on the drive, and Chris and

Paul Richmond were the same age, and Faustino Mendietta, only seventeen, was also going. Plus, Chris would be a lot cheaper than a hired hand.

Belissari shook his head. Chris seemed well on his way to manhood. That was a problem out here. Boys didn't have enough time to be boys. Chris had been doing a man's share of work for years now, and Buddy Pecos had been right. The kid had the makings of a fine cowboy, could sit in a saddle all day, was easy to like, and never shirked his duties—and he liked working cattle.

Why anyone would, Pete just couldn't fathom.

"When's Pete coming back home, Mama Hannah?" Cynthia asked.

Hannah shook her head. "He has to break a lot of horses for Mr. Cale, dear," she answered. She brushed a stray lock of auburn hair of the girl's forehead.

"Will he come back before y'all go to Kansas?" Angelica asked.

"Of course."

They were eating on the patio, waiting for the cowboys to come in for their share of the noon grub. Cale had elected to start the roundup at Hannah's ranch, and since his chuckwagon cook was late, Hannah had been forced to do all of the cooking. She watched as the crew rode up to the corrals.

"Hurry up," she told quiet Bruce. The boy looked up with his permanently sad eyes. "So the cowboys can eat."

The boy didn't have to be told again. He finished the last of his beans, mumbled an "excuse me," and ran back to the cabin. The dusty cowhands must be a frightening lot to him, Hannah thought, as she rose and began collecting the dishes.

Angelica helped, grabbing a handful of tin cups. "Do y'all have to go to Kansas, Mama Hannah?" the girl asked.

"Yes, honey, we do. But you'll like Mr. Lake, and he'll be able to teach you a lot more than I can."

"But it's so far."

Hannah nodded.

"Hey!" Paco shouted. "Maybe you and Pete can get married in Dodge City!"

Hannah blushed. Her embarrassment turned to anger when one of the cowboys hooted. "Married!" the sunburned Texan said. "Boy, men don't get married in Dodge City. They—"

"Shut up, Dunson," Cal Maddox snapped. "You got no more sense than an owlhead. Allow me, ma'am," Cale's foreman added and collected the stack of plates from Hannah's arms.

The man called Dunson glared at Maddox briefly before his eyes locked on Hannah. She met his stare until the Texan mumbled something and moved to the pot of stew.

"Help yourself, gentlemen," she told the dirty cowboys. "I have another pot of coffee in the cookshed."

They dumped the dirty dishes in the wreck pan by the shed, and Hannah went inside to fetch the coffeepot. Angelica whispered, "I don't like that tall fella. He didn't even wash his hands before eating."

Hannah thought the girl was speaking to her, but when she turned around she saw Cal Maddox nodding and placing his right hand on Angelica's shoulder.

"Don't pay him no mind, missy," Maddox said. The cowboy suddenly jerked his hand away and stared. "What on earth is that?"

"What?" Angelica backed away.

Maddox knelt and gingerly brushed the girl's hair away from her ear. "Be very, very still," he whispered and reached tentatively, then jerked his hand away so fast that Angelica—and Hannah—jumped.

"There!" Maddox said. "Got it." He opened his fist. "Wonder how that got there?"

Angelica giggled and plucked a bright green marble from the cowboy's palm. "Look, Mama Hannah! It was magic." She turned back to face the cowboy. "Can I keep it?"

Maddox grinned. "It was in your ear, missy." And he slowly straightened as Angelica ran into the cabin, yelling for the other children to come and see.

Hannah stepped outside. Maddox tipped his hat and took the pot from her hands.

"You're very kind," she said.

The cowboy scoffed. "There's some that will disagree with you, Miss Scott."

"How long had you planned that trick?"

Maddox smiled. "It just come to me right then. Never been one to think things through, ma'am. Like now . . ."

Hannah felt chilled as Maddox's right hand reached toward her. Her stomach quivered, but she couldn't move. Cal's eyes were hypnotic, like a rattlesnake's. She closed her eyes as his fingers brushed her hair.

"Got it!" he yelled.

Hannah's eyes shot open. She looked at the balled fist in front of her and laughed like a schoolgirl. Slowly Cal opened his fist. It wasn't a marble he held, but a small, pink pearl.

"I think this belongs to you, ma'am," he said.

Hannah's head shook firmly. The childish feelings she had felt earlier disappeared. "I don't think so, Mr. Maddox."

"It was your ear, missy."

Hannah felt anger, not amusement.

"Ma'am, it ain't much. I fetched it out of a mussel from the middle branch of the Concho down near Saint Angela. It don't mean a thing. Keep it, Miss Scott. Give it to one of them pretty girls when they're of age."

Her face remained stern.

"You'd be doin' me a favor, ma'am. Them other waddies find out I got a war bag full of Concho River pearls, they won't let me hear the end of it till I'm six feet under."

Her resolve wilted underneath his ever-present smile. She took the small jewel, fingering it gently. "Thank you, Mr. Maddox," she said and slipped the pearl into her skirt pocket.

"No need for thanks, Miss Scott. I'd best be gettin'

back to them boys with this coffee. Be seein' you, ma'am.''

The wagon was a typical hundred-dollar Studebaker with a chuck box on the end, water barrel on the left side and toolbox on the right. The heavy tarp had been rolled up and tossed on the bed, revealing ropes, empty sacks, and a chain attached to the bottom of the bent-wood bows. Hannah had seen chuckwagons like it all over Texas, but never the fancy lettering painted in gold on the hinged lid of the chuck box.

Lord, what fools these mortals be!

The driver set the brake, praised his team of mules, and dropped to the dusty ground. Spotting Hannah, he swiped off a wide-brimmed, dust-covered Boss of the Plains, revealing long brown hair with a shock of silver over his temples as he bowed. He sported a graying mustache and underlip beard and wore black trousers tucked into well-worn Cavalry boots and a bright yellow brocade vest over a dark blue shirt and black striped tie.

"J. W. Dougherty," he said. He had no accent. He could hail from Maine or Monterey or anywhere in between. Dougherty extended a bony hand but quickly brought it back. Hannah had no way of shaking hands; both hands held up her skirt, which she was using as a makeshift basket to carry a dozen eggs.

Hannah introduced herself and gestured at his quotation.

"Most chuck wagons have their outfit's brand," she said. "Yours has Shakespeare."

Dougherty's gray eyes brightened. "You're a well-schooled woman, Miss Scott. Most of the saddle tramps I cook for believe I'm also a circuit-riding Methodist minister and that quotation comes from the Holy Bible. One fool thought it was Stonewall Jackson's dying words."

"There's usually a troupe stopping in town once or twice a year," she explained. "I enjoy it when they perform Shakespeare." She didn't see any reason to explain that she often didn't understand a word they were saying, nor that she recognized the words on the wagon only because one acting company had performed *A Midsummer Night's Dream* last December.

Dougherty shook his head and collected a handful of eggs. "Miss Scott," he said, "when Julian Cale wired me that a woman would be driving the hoodlum wagon, I thought the man mad. But now I look forward to this particular trail drive. I freely admit that I am in love with you." He stepped back, knelt, and said: " 'Shall I compare thee to a summer's day? Thou art move lovely and more temperate.' "

Hannah had met a few trail cooks before. They were crusty, ill-tempered men, many of them stoved-up cowhands who couldn't work cattle anymore. They were called "belly cheaters, grease burners, grub spoilers" or worse, and often with good reason. But she figured that if J. W. Dougherty cooked as well as he charmed, they would be in good hands.

"Don't break the eggs, Mr. Dougherty," she said and turned to walk back to the cookshed.

Pete Belissari lowered himself into the tub of hot water in Cale's bunkhouse. Faustino handed him a scrub brush, laughed, and hurried out the door. Pete closed his eyes and let the water warm his body and soothe his cuts and bruises. He had pulled a muscle in his left thigh, lost a thumbnail, sprained a couple of fingers on his right hand, and dislocated his left shoulder once—but there were no broken bones.

For weeks, he had seen nothing but Julian Cale's rough string and Faustino Mendietta. The boy had been a lot of help, and would come in handy on the trail drive. Now the crew had moved to round up Cale's cattle, and Pete had finally ridden the last of the horses to a standstill. Some of the mounts were still green and a bit skittish, but nothing a good cowboy couldn't handle.

A door opened, and Pete smelled fried chicken. His mouth watered and his stomach growled. J. W. Dougherty cooked up the best meals around, even better than Hannah, and Pete wasn't a slouch behind a skillet himself.

"What was that you told me once? 'Too much rest becomes a pain.' " Julian Cale's voice resonated in the small building. Pete's eyes opened. A wad of chewing tobacco stretched Cale's cheek like wet leather. His jaws worked ferociously, then the rancher turned and sent a stream of brown juice across the room. It splattered on the wall just above the brass spittoon at which he had aimed. Cale didn't seem to care that he had missed.

"I didn't say that," Belissari said tiredly. "Homer did. And he never worked for you."

The rancher stopped chewing and smiled. He wiped his mouth with the back of his hand. "Mendietta's boy says you've finished with the remuda."

Belissari nodded. "For the most part, but none of them is snuffy. I doubt if they'd even throw you."

Cale mumbled, "I see." His teeth attacked the tobacco once more. "You probably would like to go see Hannah, maybe sleep a couple of days before we hit the trail."

Pete said nothing, though the thought wasn't foreign to him.

"Well, you can't, Mr. Bronc Peeler. We're moving out for Dodge at first light."

Chapter Five

"**I** don't like mixed herds," Buddy Pecos told Julian Cale before dawn broke that morning. "They spook too easily, plus you gotta worry 'bout some heifer dropping a calf. I'd rather drive only beeves."

"So would I," Cale replied, "but this is what we've got. Twenty-six hundred head, bulls, cows, and steers."

Pecos grunted and handed a coffee cup to Belissari, who had just stepped outside the bunkhouse. "Mornin'," he said soberly.

Pete stared into the black sky where just a trace of gray could be found in the east. "I'll have to take your word for it," he said.

Cale emptied the dregs from his cup onto the ground and nodded toward the corral. "I want you and the

Mendietta boy to do all the roping, Belissari. A waddie tells you which horse he wants, y'all fetch him. Nobody else swings a reata in the remuda. Afterward, the boy will ride drag and you'll push the horse herd. Don't let the remounts get too close to the cattle. Longhorns scare easier than a baby girl.''

Belissari nodded, drained the already cold coffee, and moved to the corral, where Faustino stood waiting with two lariats in his hands. This part seemed easy. A cowhand would amble to the corral, pick out a mount from his string, and either Pete or Faustino would catch the horse. The cowhand did the saddling.

Belissari heard the jingling of trace chains and saw the chuck wagon roll out of the ranch yard. He expected Hannah to follow, but Dougherty's Studebaker traveled alone.

''Where's Hannah?'' Pete asked. In the dim glow of lantern light, he saw Faustino shrug.

''She's sayin' good-bye to the young'uns,'' Pecso answered. ''Supposed to meet us by the herd. Fetch me Black Betty, pard.'' The tall cowhand grinned. ''You know, Pete, I'm gonna enjoy givin' you orders.''

Belissari shook out a loop and moved through the thick mass of horses. He made out the dark mare with a white snip. Black Betty made no effort to run, so Pete slipped the rope over her neck and led her outside the corral.

''I'll ride my dun,'' Sergeant Major Cadwallader ordered. Pete turned back to the corral but Faustino whispered, *''Con permiso.''* Belissari nodded, and the

smiling teenager dipped underneath a rail to rope Cadwallader's mount.

Pete thought about Hannah. He hadn't seen her in
weeks. At least she got to say good-bye to the kids.
They'd be upset with him. Well, he hoped they liked
him enough that they would be unhappy he didn't visit
before leaving for three, maybe four, months. He promised himself he'd bring them something from Kansas.

"Rope OL' Huck Finn for me, Pete."

Belissari stared at Irwin Sawyer. The blond-haired,
blue-eyed oaf spoke with his mouth full of Dougherty's
sourdough biscuits. "Which one's Huck Finn?" Pete
asked.

Sawyer chewed for a second, then spit out his answer along with a few bits of food. "Liver chestnut
with the white face and forelegs." The young cowboy
swallowed the last of the biscuits. "We're burnin'
daylight."

Pete frowned. He'd also have to take orders from
Sawyer and Cal Maddox, at least when roping horses.
It was going to be a long way to Dodge City.

The sun dipped over the eastern mountains, and
Hannah finally saw the herd stretched out in the valley
for what seemed like more than a mile. The longhorns
were a mixed lot of colors and types, but she recognized El Moro, now road-branded with Cale's Double
Rail C, at the front of the herd. That didn't surprise
her. The ugly longhorn would lead the herd, and make
any young bull regret challenging him.

Only she and Beto Mendietta had elected to accompany Cale on the cattle drive. Most had sent a hundred or so head, taking his price of fifteen dollars. Two decided to join Milton Faver's outfit, and a few more wanted to wait out the drought and pray for the best. Luke Wilkinson sold his ranch and all of his property, sent his small herd to Fort Worth by the railroad at Marfa—at a fortune in shipping costs—and moved back east in defeat.

She wouldn't, couldn't, be like Wilkinson. Nor would she gamble on West Texas weather or sell cheaply. *Oh, God*, she prayed, *I hope I'm doing right*.

Bedrolls, war bags, tack, and a few other supplies filled the bed in her wagon. She recognized Pete's belongings and wondered how he was doing. Cal Maddox's war bag leaned against Pete's bedroll, and she remembered the Concho River pearl, tucked away in a cash box and hidden underneath a rock in her barn. She felt guilty again.

Buddy Pecos had driven the hoodlum wagon, his saddle mount tethered to back of the wagon, to her ranch yesterday afternoon. The children attacked him, Darcy peppered him with kisses, and Desmond and Paco forced him to play an inning of baseball. Hannah had laughed until her ribs hurt. And she thought she swung the bat poorly and ran the bases like a baby javelina.

Afterward, she expressed her displeasure that Pete had neglected the children. Even Chris came by the day before to say his farewell.

"You know how Julian Cale is," Pecos argued. "He'll work Pete so hard till there ain't nothin' left of him but saddle sores and sinew."

Hannah frowned. "Even Cal Maddox came by, and he barely knows these children."

Pecos's cold eye turned even icier. He pulled his hat down lower. "Maddox," he said in a tone neither accusatorial nor curious, but far from friendly.

"He's a nice man, Buddy." Hannah felt as if she had to explain something, and that made her angry at Buddy, at Pete, at herself. "The children have taken to him."

"He's a cow*boy*, Hannah," Pecos said firmly and mounted his horse. Buddy didn't need to add what he was thinking: And Pete's a horse*man*.

The sound of another wagon interrupted her thoughts. J. W. Dougherty pulled the chuck wagon beside her and set the brake. A hawk cried in the morning air and flew over the herd. " 'One touch of nature makes the whole world kin,' " he said, sweeping off his Stetson and bowing from the driver's seat. "A beautiful morning, Miss Scott. Are you ready?"

"Yes, Mr. Dougherty. I believe I am."

The cook released the brake. "Then let us go to Kansas." He whipped the team of mules with his reins and pulled in front of her wagon, reciting at the top of his lungs:

> *"Over the Mountains*
> *Of the Moon,*

> *Down the Valley of the Shadow,*
> *Ride, boldly ride,"*
> *The Shade replied,—*
> *"If you seek for Eldorado."*

"More Shakespeare?" Hannah called out.

"Edgar Allan Poe, my dear. I don't want you to think my repertoire is limited to the Bard."

By midday, Pete estimated he had eaten two pounds of dust that tasted like the south end of more than two thousand northbound cattle and horses. And he figured the boys riding drag, Chris, Faustino, Paul Richmond, and Irwin Sawyer, had swallowed three times as much. The drag riders fell at the rear of the herd and kept the slower animals moving. Off to the side, Pete couldn't even see those poor waddies because of the cloud of white dust.

Farther up rode the flank men, Andy Dunson with his massive handlebar mustache and Chito Ruthven, Beto Mendietta's taciturn Scottish-Mexican hired hand. Beto himself rode at the flank, by the swelling herd, opposite Sergeant Major Cadwallader. At the point, leading the herd, were Cal Maddox and Buddy Pecos.

They stopped around noon for remounts and coffee and bacon, then pushed on. Pete only had time for a quick hello to Hannah and even quicker meal before he and Faustino were back by the horses, collecting fresh mounts for every cowhand.

A brutal sun baked his face and head, but at least

the horses remained cooperative. He couldn't say the same about the longhorns. Twice, a steer bolted to the left just in front of the remuda. Both times, Cadwallader, now riding Crockhead, cut off the *grulla* and sent it back to the herd. Pete couldn't decide which impressed him more: Cadwallader's skill as a cowboy, or Crockhead's improvement as a cow horse.

Julian Cale had ridden off ahead to scout the trail and water. When he finally returned, Belissari figured they would stop soon and bed down the herd. Sadly, he was mistaken. The rancher, now trail boss, barked a couple of orders to Dougherty and Hannah, and the two wagons picked up the pace and soon disappeared from the slow-moving herd. Afternoon faded, the sun dipped behind the mountains and brought needed cool relief. But Cale kept the herd moving, and they didn't stop until after dusk.

Pete and Faustino put together a makeshift rope corral for the remuda, using poles to keep the collection of lariats about four feet high, and brought out night horses for each cowboy, staking each mount behind the chuck wagon. Pete chose Poseidon for his night horse. He had brought only two of his personal horses along, the gray mustang he would trust with his life, and Dardanus. Lightning Flash and Duck Pegasus were great racers, strong, intelligent animals, but they weren't cow horses, so they stayed in Hannah's corral. He slipped Poseidon a sugar cube and patted his neck. Finally, he found a blue enamel plate and tin cup and moved down the chuck line.

Supper was red bean pie, bacon, and sourdough biscuits. Belissari studied his plate. Two thousand six hundred head of cattle grazed just a few hundred yards away, and there wasn't a speck of beef to eat. He filled his cup with strong coffee and found a seat beside Buddy Pecos.

"How many miles did we make?" he asked his friend.

Having finished supper, except for his second cup of coffee, Buddy was busy with the makings of a cigarette. He nodded, letting Pete know he had heard the question, but didn't answer until the smoke was lit and he had enjoyed a deep pull.

"Twelve miles," Pecos finally answered. "Cale wanted to push 'em hard so they might be too tired to spook. We'll slow down after a couple of days."

Slow down! Pete shook his head. Snakes crawled faster than this. Forking some of the mashed and baked pinto beans into his mouth, expecting the worst, Belissari should have known better. He could taste the nutmeg and vanilla. Even the bacon had been cooked perfectly. A meal like this should be savored, Belissari thought, but he was just too hungry. He wolfed down the meal and drained the cup of Arbuckles before Pecos finished his smoke.

"Where's Hannah?" Pete asked.

Buddy flicked the stub of his cigarette into the fire. "Sleepin'," he said. "You'd best catch a few winks your ownself."

With a groan, Pete struggled to his feet and slowly

moved to the chuck wagon, dropping his dishes into the wreck pan. He found Dougherty replenishing his sourdough starter at the chuck box.

"Excellent meal, Mr. Dougherty," he said. "A man with your many talents should be in New York or San Francisco, not the Davis Mountains heading up the Western Trail."

"Flattery," the cook said and slid the jar into a cubbyhole in the box. "You speak nothing but flattery, and the gospel truth. And that, Mr. Belissari, will take you places. Have a cigar." Dougherty pulled a long cheroot from his bright vest.

Pete ran the cigar under his nose, bit off an end, and lit it from the lantern on top of the chuck box. This wasn't some cheap stogie from a Fort Davis saloon, but a well-made, rich treat. Dougherty found a cheroot for himself.

" 'I were but little happy, if I could say how much,' " Pete said.

The cook's eyes danced with joy. "Mr. Belissari," he said. "Here I am thinking that you were schooled only in *The Odyssey* and *The Iliad,* and you amaze me with your taste. *Much Ado About Nothing.* I am indeed impressed."

Pete smiled and found his bedroll. He smoked only a quarter of the cigar before letting it go out and sticking the rest in his shirt pocket. He hit the ground with a sigh and fell asleep in minutes only to be awakened later by the violently trembling ground.

He sat up quickly, eyes adjusting to the black sky.

Recognition hit suddenly, and he was moving to the horses staked by the chuck wagon even before he heard Beto Mendietta's piercing scream:

"Stam-pede!"

Chapter Six

Hannah sat upright in the bed of the hoodlum wagon. Chains rattled, axles creaked, and horses and men screamed. The ground shook. In the dim glow of the lantern on the chuck wagon, she made out Pete as he fought to control a rearing, snorting Poseidon. Another form swung into a saddle and charged toward her. "Stay here!" he commanded, raked the flanks of his horse with his spurs, and disappeared into the darkness. Seconds passed before she realized it had been Cal Maddox.

She realized suddenly what was happening. *Stampede.* Pete had finally calmed the gray mustang long enough to slip his left foot in the stirrup, then Poseidon shied and took several quick steps away from the chaos as men tried to mount their night horses and race to the herd. Hannah gasped as Pete's leg shot up and he fell hard onto his back, moccasin wedged in the stirrup.

Flinging off the bedroll, she leaped over the wagon's side and sprinted as Poseidon dragged Pete a few yards before stopping. Belissari raised both hands and pleaded with the horse to "Whoa." Surprisingly, the frightened mustang obeyed. Suddenly someone grabbed the bridle and drew the horse close. Pete pulled his foot loose and climbed in the saddle.

"Thanks," he told Chris.

The boy smiled and mounted his own horse.

Hannah had stopped. A man galloped by her again and shouted, "Belissari. You and Mendietta take care of the remuda! The rest of you loafers, let's ride!" Julian Cale, Hannah thought. Chris galloped past her. She raised her hand, wanted to tell him to be careful, but he didn't see her. And just like that they were gone, the rumbling of the earth faded and she stood alone.

She wrung her hands and bit her lip. Something popped to her left, and she turned. Someone knelt by the dying embers of the campfire, stirring the coals while adding dry grass and kindling. Orange flame leapt to life, revealing the weary face of J. W. Dougherty. He waited until the fire burned steadily before adding two pieces of cedar.

"Morning," he said. "Best get the coffee on."

Hannah cleared her throat. "What do we do now?"

"Well, we don't just sit around and wait. See if you can't find some more wood. I'll get the breakfast ready. The boys'll be grouchy if they get back and there's nothing to eat."

Hannah shook her head. She looked for the Big Dipper, but clouds obscured the stars, so she had no idea what time it was. Using the lantern, she picked her way through the cedar brakes and gathered an armload of firewood before returning to the campfire. There, J. W. Dougherty handed her a cup of steaming black coffee. He mumbled something. Too early for Shakespeare, she guessed.

The quiet night frightened her more than the terrifying sounds of the stampede. She worried about Chris. Too many times cowboys in Fort Davis had told stories about friends being caught under the hooves, being trampled to death and so disfigured that they could only be recognized by their boots, spurs, or the pattern of their shirts.

"At least they're running north," Dougherty said as he mixed batter in a bowl.

Hannah placed the coffee cup aside. "I thought Mr. Cale said if we pushed them hard the first few days, they wouldn't stampede."

"Cows sometimes see things differently. You want to go back home?"

"No," she snapped. "I don't like just sitting here."

Dougherty put the bowl at his feet, reached into a nearby sack and tossed her a potato. "Then peel this. That'll keep you busy. Knife's in the chuck box."

She rose and found the knife. "How can you make breakfast?" she asked. Her tone was curious, not angry.

"You get used to it, Hannah. I went up the trail for

the first time back in '74 to Chetopa. Nobody remembers Chetopa anymore, but she saw her share of longhorns. Never made it to Abilene, but I've seen the elephant in Ellsworth, Wichita, Great Bend, Caldwell, Dodge City and even Baxter Springs. What I'm saying, Hannah, is that this is old hat to me. Unless the herd's heading straight for camp, I just take my time, and let all those cowboys do the running.''

Hannah sat across from Dougherty and smiled. Bootless, his socks barely covered his feet, his suspenders weren't fastened, and bacon grease stained his pink longjohn shirt. He definitely didn't resemble the dapper-dressed gentleman who usually sat in the chuckwagon reciting Shakespeare monologues or Poe's or Dryden's poetry.

She felt better now, relaxed. Hannah giggled. ''Your fly's unbuttoned, Mr. Dougherty,'' she said.

They rode in well after sunrise, a haggard bunch with dirty faces and red-rimmed eyes. Many of them were barely dressed. Chito Ruthven wore only his boots, sombrero, and longjohns; young Paul Richmond hadn't even pulled on his boots. She let out a sigh and prayer when she spotted Chris. He reined his dun in front of her and smiled.

''I reckon those mossy horns figured they hadn't traveled enough for one day,'' he said cheerfully.

Where did he hear that? Hannah mused. Buddy Pecos maybe. Or Cal Maddox. That sounded like something they would say.

"Hungry?" she asked.

"Yes, Mama—er, yes ma'am, but I got to find Pete and get another mount. I also need to tell him not to give me a white horse for a night mount no more."

"Any more. Why?"

"Cal Maddox says a white horse attracts lightning. I'll see you."

She looked up after Chris had gone and searched the faces. Buddy and Cal weren't there, nor was Beto. Before she could ask, Julian Cale dismounted in front of her and handed the reins to his nephew.

"Take this nag to the remuda, if you can find it, and bring back two fresh mounts. Then you can grab a bite to eat, after you've found your boots, Paul."

He shook his head disgustedly as the youth rode out of camp. "I sleep in my boots when I'm on a drive," he said. "Boy's got a lot to learn about cowboying."

"He's just a boy, Mr. Cale."

"Yes'm."

She cleared her throat. "How bad was it?"

Cale shrugged and shook his head. "Not bad, really. Sawyer was night-herding with Mendietta. Says he barely sneezed and the whole herd took off. Just felt like running, I reckon. They didn't scatter too much, don't think we lost that many. We turned them and got them milling without too much trouble. Maddox, Pecos, and old man Mendietta are with them now."

Andy Dunson handed him a cup of coffee. Cale took it without thanks and sipped. "Well," the rancher said.

"If they keep running like this, we might shorten our trip to Dodge City by two or three weeks."

It figured, Belissari thought. One horse had bolted from the rope corral that night before he and Faustino managed to keep the others from—what was the saying?—lighting a shuck for parts unknown. One horse.

Dardanus.

He had left the young Mexican with the remuda at sunrise and took off on Poseidon in search of the runaway gelding. Two canyons and one rattlesnake later, he had found the horse munching on grama grass in the shade just happy as you please. He slipped a reata over Dardanus's neck and led the gelding back to camp, where just about everything awaited him: a lecture from Chris on what constitutes a good night horse, a lecture from Julian Cale about not going off looking for some ridge-running claybank when horses were cheap but cattle paid the creditors, and some banter from Cadwallader and Chito Ruthven on the proper way to mount a horse.

"How's your ankle?" Hannah asked.

Belissari shrugged. "I'm all right." He rubbed his hindquarters. "At least I landed on my brains." Actually, when his foot slid up in the stirrup he had hit the ground on his back so hard he knew he would be sporting a massive bruise all the way to Kansas. Still, it had been his pride that hurt more. After all, he was the wrangler, a professional horseman, yet it had been his foot caught in the stirrup, and if Poseidon had not been halfway obedient, or if Chris hadn't thought fast enough to grab the bridle, the remains of Pete Belissari might be scattered on every yucca plant and prickly pear between here and Marfa.

''Don't fret,'' Cadwallader told him. ''These cattle have probably run enough to satisfy them. Doubt if they'll stampede again until they're running up the chutes in Dodge on their way to the Kansas City slaughterhouse.''

And it seemed the old sergeant major was right. The next few days seemed routine. They came out of the Davis Mountains and moved toward Fort Stockton. Pete glanced back toward home. In the dust, the rugged peaks resembled ocean waves in rough seas. ''The wine-dark sea,'' Homer had written. He hadn't realized how much he loved these mountains. He sighed and pulled up his bandanna to fend off the smothering dust. A barren, blistering wasteland stretched out before him.

They would move past Fort Stockton and on up past San Angelo, converging on the Western Trail at the Colorado River. John T. Lytle had blazed that trail a dozen or so years ago when he sent thirty-five hundred longhorn to Nebraska. Since '79, the Western Trail, Dodge City Trail, Fort Griffin Trail, whatever you wanted to call it, had been the main route for the northbound herds.

From the Colorado, they'd drive through the prairie country, past Albany, the abandoned Fort Phantom Hill and the wicked little town called The Flat near Fort Griffin on the Clear Fork of the Brazos. Afterward, it was a simple little swim across the Brazos, a bath in the Pease, and on to Doan's Crossing on the Red River, north through the Indian Nations and a skip across western Kansas to Dodge City.

Easy as scrambled eggs. *Yeah,* Pete thought, and *Odysseus's journey was also a "vacation."*

Dust burned her eyes, the wind blistered her lips and the sun baked her scalp. Hannah figured she had gained ten pounds on the drive, and it had nothing to do with J. W. Dougherty's cooking. No, it felt like six pounds of dirt caked her dress, another three cushioned her boots and the remainder could be found in her hair. She pulled the wagon beside Dougherty's Studebaker and set the brake.

Dougherty held a sack of dried manure—wood was scarce for fuel here—and swept the Stetson off his sweaty head with his free hand and bowed. " 'She walks in beauty, like the night. Of cloudless climes and starry—' "

Hannah stuck out her tongue. The cook laughed. "Lord Byron," he credited. "I've been waiting days to use his poem. I deduced that the time was right."

"Yeah."

"Perhaps, I can make amends if you found my joke humorless." Hannah concentrated on unhitching the team. Dougherty continued. "I asked Faustino to saddle a horse for you. A mile north is an old spring. Comanche used to hide out there, but the water is cool, and the spring is large and deep enough for a nice, refreshing bath."

Hannah looked up. Dougherty lowered the basket

and replaced his hat. "I know what you're thinking, Hannah. You're saying that my classical monologues can't hide my roguish nature, that a thespian can't be trusted, especially one with a sack full of dung. But fear not. I shan't be able to accompany you, or spy on you. I have vinegar pie and sourdough biscuits to make by sundown."

Hannah said, "Finish with the team, Mr. Dougherty, please," and went to find Faustino.

She slid off the saddle by the spring and laughed, placing her right hand in the dark, smelly mud that covered the ground. Parts of the spring had already dried into cracked, hard earth. No bath. Not here. *Poor J.W. Dougherty will be so disappointed.* She wiped off the mud on her skirt, mounted the dapple mare, and rode back to camp.

The horse reared. Hannah screamed and landed hard on her side. *Rattlesnake!* flashed through her mind as the mare turned and loped back toward the mudhole. Then she felt the ground, and realized it wasn't a snake that had spooked the horse. She blinked away the dust and sweat and saw them coming. Sunlight danced across their shiny horns, hooves thundered, and a terrifying balling carried across the sun-baked prairie.

Two thousand six hundred stampeding longhorns pounded their way toward her.

Chapter Seven

She slipped once attempting to rise, then scrambled to her feet and ran as hard as she could, trying to get out of the path of the wild-eyed herd that seemed to stretch a hundred miles. The ground shook. Cattle bellowed. The sound of the trampling hooves intensified. She knew she would never make it.

"Hannah!"

The voice barely carried over the din of the stampede. Hannah kept running. To stop and turn meant death under the hooves. Her lungs burned. Dust stung her eyes. Pounding hooves drew closer, and she tried to run faster but her boots weren't accommodating. She felt hot breath on her neck. She closed her eyes and screamed—too terrified to pray.

Something gripped her waist and suddenly she was

lifted—*Elijah being taken up to heaven in a whirlwind* shot through her mind—and her stomach slammed into the side of something hard. The jarring motion of a galloping horse and a strong arm almost crushing the breath from her lungs forced her eyes open. Her vision blurred. All she saw was dust. All she smelled was the sweat of a horse.

"Hang on!" the voice commanded.

Hannah's vision cleared enough to make out the saddle horn. She reached up with her right hand and clung to it for life. Her left hand tried to wrap around the rider's waist but she couldn't make it. Instead, her fingers slid inside a leather gun belt, and she pulled on it until the metallic casings of the cartridges bit into her palm. But she wasn't about to let go.

Pete? she thought. No, she could feel the tips of boots against her legs, and Pete always wore moccasins. She craned her neck and looked up. His gray hat had flown off, and the wind made his curly hair dance. Clenched teeth set Cal Maddox's jaw firm, and his eyes blazed with determination.

"Yeah!" he shouted in triumph and relief, and the roar of the herd passed. They were safe, but Maddox kept riding hard to put a little distance between them and the longhorns. He started to rein in his lathered gelding.

Hannah felt her fingers slipping.

"Cal!" she cried.

He jerked the horse to a stop. Hannah grabbed his outstretched left arm with her right, and pulled on his gun belt. In a blink, the look on Cal's face changed. His eyes widened with fear and suddenly he was coming out of the saddle. Hannah felt herself falling, not that it was much of a drop from the side of a Texas cow pony, but a hundred-and-sixty-five-pound cowhand was coming down on top of her.

Hannah screamed.

Cal Maddox said, "Oh—" but the splattering of mud drowned out his profanity as the two tumbled into the gooey, smelly remains of the old Comanche spring.

The gelding snorted, as if laughing, and Cal rolled over. Hannah sat up and pulled her hands up through the sucking, thick mud. Her hair was filthy, as well as her face, and she looked at her soiled clothes. Cal Maddox spit out a mouthful of the slop and stood, shaking off mud from his right hand, which he extended.

Hannah reached up. Maddox pulled and tried to step back, but the mud gripped the cowboy's left boot like a vise. He groaned and pulled harder. There was a slight sucking noise, and then both went sailing back into the old watering hole—with Cal Maddox's boot still in place.

Maddox swore again. Hannah pushed herself off him this time, and sat back as the cowboy sat up. His hands disappeared into the black crud and pulled off a once-white sock now blackened and thick with mud. He balled up the sock and tossed it into his empty boot.

His eyes locked on Hannah. Wind carried the dust from the stampede over them, covering them with another layer of dirt. She closed her eyes until the dust passed, and then looked at her savior. Cal Maddox sat in the mud, elbows on his knees, chin in his hands, painted in dust and mud like a circus clown.

Hannah placed a muddy hand over her mouth and tried to suppress a giggle. Mistake. She spit out a chunk of wet earth.

"Nice bath, huh?" Maddox said.

She fell back, sinking into the smelly pit, staring up at the blue sky, not caring. Hannah grabbed a handful of mud and tossed it at Maddox. She felt Cal's return shot land underneath her chin.

Hannah laughed, and Cal Maddox chimed in. They cackled and threw mud at each other until it hurt to breathe.

Pete brought her plate and coffee that night. Hannah still smelled a tad—well, more than that, actually— sour after her mud bath. He knelt beside her, told her that the herd stampeded because, they guessed, a sudden breeze carried the scent of a dead skunk. He sipped his coffee.

"How are you feeling?" he asked.

"Better than I smell," she replied. She looked across the camp at Cal Maddox, who also had found a place away from the others to eat his dinner in smelly silence.

She remembered the mud hole, when they had finished laughing, Cal pulling her to her feet and her slipping and falling against his muddy chest. She looked up at him, and felt her stomach knot. He brushed away her muddy hair and smiled. Hannah thought he might kiss her then. Now she wondered if she would have let him. He hadn't thought. He pulled away and found his muddy boot and sock.

"We best catch up with the herd," he said, and they rode double a couple of miles until they found the long-horns peacefully grazing as if nothing had happened.

Pete Belissari was solid, safe, well-liked, well-educated, and respected in the community. Hannah respected him, and he treated her as an equal, with respect. Respect went a long way in Hannah's way of thinking. Yet Pete could also be mule-headed, and half the time she thought he might rather be in the middle of the wilderness chasing wild horses than at home with her. She loved him? Yes, she couldn't deny that, and he loved her. But was he always there for her? Would he always be around? Of that, she wasn't so sure, especially considering some of their recent fights. He might just saddle Poseidon and ride off after a herd of mustangs.

Of course, Hannah couldn't blame Pete for everything. She had also been called stubborn, temperamental and testy. Working on a ranch, tending the children, running that stagecoach line—all of that left her tired, with little time for herself, or Pete, and more determined to succeed in what everybody seemed to call "a man's world."

Cal Maddox was dashing, fun, and charming. He did things on the spur of the moment, seldom thought a situation through, whereas Pete would analyze everything like a college professor before picking his path.

He made his share of mistakes, but usually his judgment hit the bull's-eye. Still, Pete had been adamant against the cattle drive, and here he was wrong. Dead wrong. And she would prove it.

"Pete?" she said.

"Yes?"

"Would you mind if I went over to Cal and ate with him? I . . . I never thanked him for saving my life."

He shook his head and rose. "I thanked him, but go ahead. I need to check on the horses anyway."

No argument. No hint of jealousy. At least he could act mad, she thought, and took her supper to the curly-haired cowboy with the war bag full of Concho River pearls.

"Mind if I sit down?" she asked.

Cal smiled, and she took a spot beside him. They ate in silence for a few minutes before she thanked him for pulling her to safety.

"No need, Hannah," he said. "I was just the closest. Besides, I was honored. It ain't every day I get to take a bath with a beautiful lady."

He stopped chewing. He looked as if he had swallowed something he shouldn't have.

"I'm sorry, ma'am. That wasn't a proper thing to say. I wasn't really thinkin'. What I mean—"

"It's all right, Cal. Besides . . ." She ran her fingers through her dirty hair. ". . . I'm not sure anyone would find me beautiful."

"They'd be blind, Hannah. And I ain't got to think that one through."

She felt uncomfortable now, so she changed the subject. "Where are you from?"

"Just 'bout everywhere," he said. "I was born in Texas, in Round Rock—that's where they killed Sam Bass—near Austin."

"Yes, I . . . I grew up in Austin." She paused, didn't want to tell him about the Travis County orphanage.

"Well, let's see," Cal continued. "I lit out from home when I was fifteen, back in '74 on my first drive. We went up the Chisholm Trail, all the way to Ellsworth. Once there, somehow I got me a job at a packin' house in Kansas City, Missouri. Did that for about six months, then me and a pal got a hankerin' to see St. Louis, so we did. Couldn't find work, so we got another notion to see Chicago. I spent, I reckon, fourteen-fifteen months up there, butcherin' Texas beef. I'd hop trains, sometimes, to work. But not in winter. No ma'am. It got mighty cold up yonder.

"Anyway, finally I got sick of that line of work, so I jumped aboard a southbound and found my way back to Kansas. Hired on in Dodge City and took some mossy horns to Wyomin'. Then I had me a notion to see the Black Hills, so me and a saddle pal rode up to Deadwood. Worked in a mine for about a month, but that didn't take to me. Got a job on a ranch outside some town in Nebraska, I forgets the name, then drifted back to Texas.

"Let's see. I've worked on ranches around Pleasanton and Junction and Jacksboro and Gonzales, and driven herds to Kansas, Nebraska, even to Las Animas,

Colorado, once, three years back. Even swept out a mercantile in Fort Worth for 'bout a week. That's the life and times of Cal Maddox in a whiskey tumbler, ma'am.''

Hannah smiled. ''No home?''

He shrugged. ''Nah. But I ain't like some of them waddies. I don't hanker to be pushin' beeves till I'm too old or stoved up to fork a saddle. I reckon I'd settle down if I had the notion . . . the money . . . and the right girl.''

Silently fuming, Belissari sent his empty coffee cup sailing toward the wreck pan. A large hand shot out and caught the tin cup before it clattered against the dirty dishes. Pete looked up into the face of a frowning Robert Cadwallader.

''That's not intelligent, Mr. Belissari,'' the old soldier said. ''You want to start another stampede?''

Pete mumbled a halfhearted apology as Cadwallader filled the cup with coffee. ''Here,'' the sergeant major said, ''hot coffee has cooled off some disorderly troopers. I imagine it'll work on a jealous mustanger.''

Belissari accepted the drink.

''It shows?''

''I'm not blind, mister. 'Jealousy is cruel as the grave: the coals thereof are coals of fire.' That's from the Song of Solomon.''

''You've been hanging around J. W. Dougherty too much.''

"You could go over and talk to the woman, Petros. You could quit acting like an old mule."

"She's a grown woman, Cad. She's not a horse with my brand." He swore softly.

"Woman on a cattle drive is a bad mistake," Cadwallader said. "Had I known this, I probably would have put in another year with the Army. The cowboy saved her life, plus he's a good-looking young man, full of vinegar, and he's not too proud to woo a gal. I'd say she just has a little crush on the boy right now. Harmless, you know? But if you keep acting like a fool, mister, you're going to have to win her back—if she'll have you."

Pete frowned as Cadwallader walked away. Belissari leaned against the chuck wagon, sipped the cup of coffee he really didn't want or need, and stared across the campfire at Hannah and Cal Maddox. *Cal.* She had called him *Cal.* Someone eased dishes into the pan and refilled a coffee cup.

"I don't care too much for that new fella, Pete," a Texan drawled. "Don't like the way he's carryin' on with Hannah."

"I don't like him either," Pete said. "But Hannah knows what she's doing. And he's a good cowhand, I guess."

"Yeah, well, maybe so. But if I was you, I'd fight him. He might have Hannah thinkin' he's a good ol' boy, but he ain't. He's just a saddle tramp, plain and simple. Be seein' you, Pete."

"Yeah. Good night." Pete followed the cowboy's bowlegged gait to his bedroll. Belissari emptied the dregs from his cup, amazed at what he had just done. He had carried on a civilized conversation, had even agreed with that Texas oaf who himself was drawn to Hannah: Irwin Sawyer.

Chapter Eight

Hannah got her bath in the Pecos River. After she had finished, so did all of the cowhands, except Chito Ruthven, who said bathing during a cattle drive brought bad fortune. Of course, it wasn't much of a bath because they had only two bars of lye soap to go around and first they pushed the cattle across Horsehead Crossing, letting the longhorns slake their thirst and muddying up the water before bedding down for the night.

"Water's low," Buddy Pecos said.

"Yeah," Julian Cale agreed.

No one felt much like talking.

Hannah vowed in the Pecos that she would toughen up. Cal Maddox had saved her life, and although that certainly beat the grim alternative, it made her feel like,

well, a girl. "Coulda happened to most anyone,"
Buddy Pecos told her. That made her feel a little better.
Heck, Poseidon had almost dragged Pete across West
Texas. Still, she realized the Western Trail stretched a
long way to Kansas, and the relentless drought and an
inexperienced trail crew, herself included, would make
this drive even harder.

They moved northwest slowly. Dougherty considered eight miles a day "a lovely jaunt." A sandstorm
held them to fewer than four miles one day, and Cale
rested the herd at a dirty water hole for a full morning
to let the cattle drink. The hole was dry when they
moved on.

Dull aches and pains, not to mention chaffed thighs
and backsides, put the crew on edge. A glaring sun in
a sky that hadn't seen a cloud in weeks didn't help
matters. After being pitched from his roan gelding one
morning, Andy Dunson took a punch at young Faustino
Mendietta. His fist missed because Pete grabbed the
Texan's arm and pushed him off balance.

"It's his fault, wrangler!" Dunson bellowed. "I
ain't gettin' my neck broke because of some sandal-
wearin' Mexican."

"He only roped the horse," Pete answered. "You
saddled him."

The two glared at each other for a minute before
Dunson spit out a mouthful of tobacco juice and
mounted the roan. Hannah still felt the tension, but Cal
Maddox strode up, chewing on a piece of jerky, and
said, "Faustino, rope the bay for me, pardner."

Hannah smiled as the young boy eagerly went back to work.

Things didn't improve much, though. Between the Middle and North Concho Rivers, Cale put the crew on water rations. Pecos sat eating his supper, talking about one drive he had been on when the herd went blind with thirst, when Beto Mendietta rode into camp.

"*Señor* Cale," the old man said. "One of *la patroña's vacas*. She has . . . dropped . . . *un ternera*, uh, a calf. I should kill it, *sí?*"

The rancher scratched his bearded chin. "No," he said. "Take my nephew. Have him kill it."

Hannah immediately searched the faces for Paul Richmond. She found him rising from his seat on the hoodlum wagon's tongue, spilling his coffee and beans, his mouth hanging open. "Me?" the boy said.

"Beto," Cale said, ignoring his nephew. "Give Paul your revolver."

"No pistola, señor."

"Well, I got one," Andy Dunson said joyfully and pulled his battered old Colt from a poorly made holster. "Here, boy, it kicks like a mule but will get the job done sure enough."

Paul Richmond's eyes filled with tears. His jaw trembled.

"Come on, kid," Dunson continued. "Beef's always better than beans, and calf brains taste mighty fine."

The teenager stepped forward tentatively. "But Uncle Julian . . ."

"Boy, I will make a man out of you, if not a cow-man. Now do as you're told. Beto!"

Hannah stood. "No," she said.

The thought of killing a calf repulsed her, but she understood its necessity. The baby would never make it, not on a trail drive. The mother might cause trouble. Better kill the animal now. But she would not stand by and let Julian Cale, good neighbor or not, bully a little boy.

Cale snapped at her. "I'm bossing this drive, Hannah Scott. You're just driving a wagon. Now—"

"It's not your calf, mister. Pete."

Pete was already moving, drawing the Remington .44 he had bought a few months back at J. B. Shields mercantile in town. He pulled the hammer to half-cock and rotated the cylinder, checking the loads. Cale's eyes burned furiously, but he kept silent.

"Mr. Belissari?"

Hannah stood dumbfounded as Paul Richmond approached Pete and held out his right hand. "Mr. Belissari, sir, I'll do it."

Pete hesitated. His Adam's apple bobbed, and he glanced at the youth first, the revolver next. The .44 snapped to full-cock, then Pete safely lowered the hammer and looked back at Richmond.

"You sure, son?"

"Yes sir."

Pete hefted the gun as if weighing his options before spinning the Remington in his hand and handing the .44 to Paul, butt forward.

"Show me the calf, Mr. Beto," the boy said, and followed the old man to the herd.

Hannah fumed all that night and the following morning. How could he? How could Pete just let a ten-year-old boy, half-crying, go kill a newborn calf just to appease his uncle?

"The boy'll be fourteen in a couple weeks, Hannah," Pecos said in a soothing tone. "And to Paul's thinkin', it sure was better to shoot the calf himself rather than some other fella do it, what with young Chris and Faustino lookin' on. Pete did all right in my book."

Maybe, Hannah thought, but conceded nothing to Buddy Pecos.

They rested for a day on the North Concho. A few of the hands wanted to ride into San Angelo, but Cale refused to allow it. "You can cool your heels in The Flat, but not before," he said before riding off to scout the trail. "If you don't like it, draw your time."

"That Cale is one miserable, iron-willed, low-down ramrod," Andy Dunson said to no one in particular, and Hannah found herself in agreement. "Only reason he'll let us see The Flat is because he needs supplies."

"Why don't you quit?" Maddox asked.

"Because I'm a dirt-poor saddle bum, just like you, Cal. Need the money. But I'll take that high-and-mighty Julian Cale down a peg or two once we get to Dodge City, mark my words. And I'll tie one hand behind my back to make it fair."

"I think I'd still bet on Mr. Cale," Chito Ruthven said with a smile, and a couple of the cowhands laughed.

Dunson kicked up dust and stormed away.

"We have some men prone to violence," J. W. Dougherty said. "After your intervention for Master Richmond, I would dare say we are close to mutiny."

"Maybe everyone will feel better once we reach the Flat," Hannah said.

"Maybe it'll rain," Dougherty said.

They saw nothing but cattle, horses, and a parched Texas until they crossed the Colorado River. There, amid the rolling plains of dry grass, they met a man traveling by buckboard from the young railroad town of Abilene to the older cowboy town of Coleman on Hords Creek.

"You boys'd be better off shipping them cattle out at Abilene than herding them to Kansas," said the traveler, a middle-aged, bald man in black broadcloth who stopped to sample J. W. Dougherty's coffee during the noon break. "I ain't felt a drop of rain in a coon's age, and they say the town of Chico is plumb out of water. Dry as an old buffalo bone."

"It'll rain," Julian Cale said.

"Suit yourself," the man replied.

They passed east of Buffalo Gap and Abilene before stopping to rest for a day near the Clear Fork of the Brazos. Hannah had lost track of the days. It could have been Monday or Sunday, May or June. She didn't know, didn't care. Cale sent Pete and Paul Richmond out hunting that morning, figuring if they could get lucky, venison might soothe a bunch of stomachs and nerves. Hannah thought Cale also assumed that a thirty-year-old wrangler and a teenage boy didn't need to rest as much as his grumpy cowhands.

She closed her eyes and let the wind blow through her knotted, dirty hair. It was the first cool breeze she had felt in weeks.

"Hey, Hannah, you feel like going for a ride?"

Hannah opened her eyes and smiled at Cal Maddox. "The last time I went for a ride, we took a mud bath after I almost got trampled to death," she said without moving. "Remember?"

"Yeah, but I can practically guarantee you these cattle are too tuckered out to move, and we're spittin' distance—beggin' your pardon—from Fort Phantom Hill. I thought you might like to see it."

She had never heard of Phantom Hill but accepted the offer if only to get away from the smell of cattle. An hour later, they dismounted and hobbled their horses near the crumbling limestone ruins of the abandoned military post.

Cal fetched a coin from his vest pocket and tossed it into the air. "Make a wish," he said as the penny dropped into an old cistern. She took a sip of water from her canteen, frowned at the brackish taste, and walked to a lone chimney that rose from the ground like a sentinel. She studied the ancient remains from a fire lay, bent, and picked up a torn doll. A gust of wind caused her to shiver.

"Kinda spooky, huh?" Cal knelt beside her. "The Army abandoned the fort long before the War, I think, then the Overland used it as a stage stop. Think some Rangers were once stationed here. Ain't much left now, though. You cold?"

She looked to the west and rose suddenly. Black clouds darkened the sky, and the wind gained intensity, bending the trees and sprouting a dust devil near one of the old foundations.

"Cal," she said. "We'd better get back."

"Yeah. We can sure use the rain, but not a twister."

They were at the horses when the first hard, icy drops pelted their hats and clothes. Before they could mount, a sheet of water soaked them. The wind moaned like a distant train. Both horses whinnied and reared. A hailstone popped Hannah's right hand, then more followed, pounding the countryside with solid white balls the size of a quarter.

"Inside!" Cal yelled and kicked open the door to a stone store magazine, jail, something. Hannah didn't care as long as the building had a roof. She and Cal pulled their horses through the door and tethered them in the back of the building.

Hannah stared out the open door. The hailstones had grown larger now, some of them the size of a man's fist. She felt Cal put his rain slicker over her shoulders.

"Reckon we're stuck," Maddox said. "We'll be safe, long as we don't get a twister. I'll try to get a fire goin'."

Hannah nodded slightly. She thought about Pete, and prayed for his safety.

Chapter Nine

"*What do you mean she's not here?*"

Pete Belissari had to shout over the vicious wind and frightened animals. He had trouble controlling Dardanus, who danced across the ground between the hoodlum wagon and Dougherty's Studebaker. Pete swore, impatient for an answer.

Irwin Sawyer shuffled his feet and tossed his spurs into the hoodlum wagon. "She and Maddox rode out this afternoon. Think they were headin' to Fort Phantom Hill." The cowhand reached into his pocket, pulled out a folding knife, and sent it sailing into the wagon bed. He shed himself of anything metal, afraid of drawing a lightning bolt.

Belissari cursed again, at himself, the spooked gelding he rode, but mostly at Cal Maddox, and looked at the approaching storm. This whole day had been a disaster. He and Paul didn't even see a scrawny jackrabbit on their hunting expedition, much less a white-tailed deer. Then Paul's bay lost a shoe, forcing Pete and the boy to ride double three miles while pulling the lame horse behind them. "I'm going after them," Belissari said.

"No you ain't!" Julian Cale bellowed. "When this storm hits, I'll need every man I have with the herd."

"I'm going after them!" Pete repeated, and kicked Dardanus into a lope.

The first blast of rain hit him near Elm Creek, which had been dry. Dardanus turned in circles, frightened by the storm's fury. Stupid, Pete thought. He should have saddled Poseidon, but there hadn't been any time. Slapping the gelding's sides with his soaked hat, Belissari forced the horse onward.

He could barely see the line of swaying oaks in front of him, maybe a hundred yards away. A hailstone cut his cheek. The wind and rain felt like ice against his drenched clothes. Dardanus reared once. Belissari swung from the saddle and pulled hard on the reins, almost having to drag the gelding to the cover of the trees.

They didn't make it.

Hailstones felt like buckshot, small at first, but steady. In less than two minutes, the ground had turned white. In less than five, the size of the hail had tripled. Before he had pulled Dardanus fifty yards, Belissari dropped to his knees, his head pounding. Giant stones pounded his sore back, head, and arms. He tasted blood. Pete forced himself up, gripping the reins, slipping once on the ice—or maybe a fist-size chunk of ice knocked him down again.

He threw himself against Dardanus, trying to soothe the bouncing, snorting green gelding, and worked on the cinch quickly. The saddle finally slid off, and Pete slapped Dardanus's rump, though there had been no need. The horse was galloping away before the saddle hit the ground.

His right wrist and hand seared with pain. Belissari had seen storms before—hurricanes growing up in Corpus Christi on the Texas Gulf, a tornado in West Texas, plenty of thunderstorms, and a couple of blizzards—but nothing like this. Groaning, he tried to lift the saddle with his right hand, but his fingers wouldn't bend. At last, using his left hand, he got the saddle up, covering his head, and half-ran, half-stumbled toward the trees.

The horses fought against their hobbles when part of the roof gave way in the far corner of the building. "It's all right," Cal said, although he had jumped more than Hannah when the weight of the hail sent a chunk of thatch and rotten timber crumbling. Cal moved to calm the horses, rubbing their necks while looking up at the ceiling, making sure the rest wasn't about to fall on their heads. Hailstones and rain fell from the opening the size of a chimney and splattered on the ruins of the roof, turning the sod floor in that corner into a bed of mud and ice.

Hannah walked away from the small fire and looked out the window. Iron bars had been set in the limestone. So this was a jail after all, guardhouse rather. In the corner of her eye, she saw Cal checking the damaged roof, kicking at the mound of ice on the dirt floor with his toe. Next, he stood beside her.

"That gave me a bit of a start myself, but I don't think any more roof will come down on us," he said. The heavy pounding died, but the wind continued its haunting howl. "There," Maddox continued. "It's stopped hailin'."

But the rain fell in torrents, being blown sideways. She felt Cal's hand on her shoulder, and she let herself be turned to face him.

"I'll take care of you, Hannah," he said. "I mean, not that you can't take care of yourself. You're a pretty special woman."

She looked at the fire, then at him. He was close. Cal Maddox leaned forward. He kissed her softly and drew back, curious maybe, wondering if she would slap him, kick him, or kiss him back. She did neither. She could have stopped him, but she let him kiss her. When he leaned forward again, however, she raised her hand.

He straightened.

"No," she said. "That wasn't right."

Cal smiled. "It sure felt right."

"I'm practically engaged."

Practically. Wasn't she engaged? She and Pete had been once, but now? Was it just understood they would get married sometime, whenever they found time. The past couple of years hadn't left much time for a wedding or honeymoon.

Cal studied her. Hannah's face showed resolve, and he frowned slightly before nodding.

"I hope you don't feel less of me, Hannah. I just . . . well . . . it just seemed. Well, I'm here for you, Hannah, if ever you need me."

"Thank you," she said and turned away.

The rain continued. She wondered how the children were doing back in Fort Davis. She thought about Pete again. And she felt guilty.

She bit her lip, closed her eyes, and steeled herself, refusing to cry.

*

The storm passed, but another quickly followed. Then another. When the series had moved southeast, it was long past midnight, so Hannah and Cal waited until dawn to return to camp. They got there quickly, but found no cattle, only a handful of horses, the chuck wagon's tarp shredded, and everyone gone except Dougherty and Cadwallader.

"Another stampede?" Cal asked after tethering the horses to the chuck wagon's tongue.

Dougherty and Cadwallader nodded. "Cattle and remuda are scattered nine ways from Sunday," the old soldier answered. "I counted fifteen dead cattle. Stopped counting after that. We lost at least a dozen horses. We're trying to round up what we can find."

Hannah asked: "Anybody hurt?"

Cadwallader frowned. "Well . . . you two . . . didn't happen to see Pete . . . did you?"

Hannah covered her mouth with both hands but said nothing. A second later, she was gathering the reins to her horse.

"Easy," Cal said. "That horse is tuckered out, Hannah. You stay here. We'll find him."

"Pete's smart. He can take care of himself." Cadwallader sounded more as though he were trying to convince himself of that.

Hannah stepped away from the gelding. She stared at Cadwallader, then Dougherty, and finally signed. Her face must have asked *What happened?* because Cadwallader cleared his throat and said, "He rode in right before the storm hit. Sawyer told him that you two went up to Phantom Hill, so he rode after you. I figured, hoped, that he caught up with you and spent the night in one of the old buildings."

"Why isn't anyone looking for him?" Her voice resonated with anger.

"We have been. Buddy Pecos rode out at first light. You all must have just missed each other. And I was just about to go make a scout. We'll find him, and I promise you he'll be fine."

Dougherty cleared his throat. "I don't know how fine he is, but there he is now." He pointed his chin.

Hannah spun around. Pete walked slowly toward them, about two hundred yards away, dragging his saddle, his shirt hanging on by ribbons.

"Think your wrist is sprained, my lad," J. W. Dougherty informed Pete. "Not broken. And your hand is pretty fairly bruised. If you were a gun man, I'd advise you not to draw on anyone for the next six weeks.''

Dougherty wrapped the black-and-blue hand and wrist with a bandanna, and pulled down the sleeve of the worn—and dry—red shirt Pete had pulled from his gear. ''Use your bandanna to keep your arm in a sling for a while.''

''Can't rope any horses with my arm in a sling,'' Pete said.

The cook laughed. ''My well-educated friend, you won't be roping any horses for a good spell, sling or no sling. I'm afraid to report the sad news that the curtain has closed on your days as our wrangler.''

Julian Cale grunted. Belissari looked at the leathery rancher. Pete leaned against the chuck wagon, and thanked Dougherty as the cook finished his doctoring and began preparing supper.

''You look a mess,'' Cale said.

''I feel worse.''

''Dougherty's right. You won't be much use to us as a wrangler from here on out. I've told Sawyer that he'll have to take over there. I figure you can still ride drag, even with one arm. You agreeable to that?''

Belissari nodded. Drag. The worst job on a cattle drive. He'd be eating dirt all the way to Dodge. Not that he had any choice. He couldn't help with the horses. He wasn't sure he would do much good at the rear of the herd.

Pete waited until Cale left before trying to pour some coffee with his left hand. The cup burned his fingers, and he sent the hot liquid sizzling against the coals, followed quickly by the tin cup. He swore underneath his breath.

"Here."

Pete turned, easing his bruised, cut back against the wagon as Hannah filled another cup and handed it to him. Using a piece of kindling, she retrieved the other cup from the fire and dropped it into the wreck pan.

Their eyes met.

"I'm sorry about Dardanus," she said softly.

Belissari nodded. He had found the gelding less than a mile from where he turned him loose, brained to death by the massive hailstones. Pete too would probably be dead if he hadn't protected his head with the forty-pound saddle and made his way to the sturdy oaks. Hannah said something else, but Pete was only half-listening. The storm left his face red from wind and cut by hail, with a large knot on the top of his head and a smaller one over his left eye. His whole body hurt. Hannah asked if he needed anything.

He wanted to say yes, to reach for her with his good hand, to pull her close. What he said, however, was this:

"How did you and Maddox enjoy your evening out?"

Hannah's blue eyes flamed. "Back up," she spat out. "We went for a ride. That's all. Don't take that tone with me. It's not my fault you're hurt. It's not my fault your horse got killed. I'm not a little girl, Pete, nor one of your mustangs. I don't need a protector. And right now, I surely don't need you."

She stormed out of camp.

Pete let out another oath and flung his cup—coffee and all—into the wreck pan. He pivoted, facing the chuck wagon, his body trembling with rage.

"Stupid!" he yelled at himself, forced his right hand into a tight fist, and sent it crashing into the Studebaker's side.

Pain dropped him to his knees. He held his throbbing right hand in front of him, gripping his arm with his left hand, grimacing, forcing back tears.

"No," J. W. Dougherty said, peering around the chuck box. "*That* was stupid."

Chapter Ten

With his right arm in an ivory-colored bandanna that served as a makeshift sling, Belissari eased off the short-coupled chestnut in silence. He had spent fourteen hours in a saddle often, sometimes more, but never behind a herd of dust-churning longhorns. Fumbling with the canteen fastened to the saddle horn, he swore at his misfortune. It took more than a minute before he could remove the cork with his left hand and wash the grit from his mouth.

"Want me to unsaddle Turk for you?" Chris asked.

"I'd appreciate it," he replied and handed the canteen to the boy. Chris took a sip, returned the cork, and went to work on the saddle. Pete felt worthless. He couldn't saddle his own horse, or cork a canteen, and

Hannah wouldn't even look at him, let alone speak to him.

"You know, Pete," Chris said, "you really should make up with Mama Hannah." The saddle hit the ground. Belissari expected more of a lecture, but the boy simply led the quarter horse to the remuda, so Belissari made his way to the chuck wagon and fell in line for supper.

J. W. Dougherty filled the tin plate with a giant biscuit, a pile of beans, and a chunk of apple cobbler. The cook looked up and asked, "Would you like me to teach you one of Shakespeare's sonnets? I have never known a sonnet to fail in the art of making up with one's true love."

Advice from a thirteen-year-old and now the cook. Belissari shook his head. What next? Pete was last in line—Chris and Faustino must still be with the horses—so he put his plate and coffee on the chuck box.

"Dougherty," he said, "there's a question I've been meaning to ask you for a long time."

"Ask away, my Greek friend."

"How did you become a cook on a trail drive?"

Laughing, J. W. removed his apron and withdrew a cigar from a drawer, bit off the end, and lit it from the nearby lantern. Once he had the tobacco fired and had exhaled a long plume of blue-gray smoke, he answered:

"All the world's a stage, my lad, and a cook in his life plays many parts." Dougherty puffed on his cigar.

"I had the misfortune of playing Falstaff in Saint Jo, Texas. Are you familiar with Falstaff?"

"*Henry IV, Part I* is my favorite play."

"By Jove, Pete, you continue to astound me. It's my favorite too. Well, I had joined up with Samuel and Sheila Corbett, and their fine thespian daughter, Lucretia, who succeeded in infatuating me as only a great actress can. The rest of our troupe included Robert Wilde, Jessie Larson, and Jedidiah James, who also drove the wagon and collected the receipts. I never should have trusted them. Any of them, but I so loved the stage.

"Anyway, the people of Saint Jo worshiped my performance, as you would expect. Falstaff appeals to the drunken, loud lot you'd find in the Cattle Drover's Saloon where we were performing since the town lacked an opera house. So after several curtain calls—there were no curtains, of course, in the saloon; we simply walked through the batwing doors and into the freezing rain—I was whisked away by some overzealous patrons—enjoying a respite, they were on a trail drive to Kansas, you see—and we sampled Saint Jo's collection of whiskey, beer, and wine. When I awoke in the town's lovely jail, with several of my new friends, the following afternoon, I found that the Corbett & Dougherty Traveling Troupe had disembarked for parts unknown, leaving behind only me and considerable debts at the hotel, restaurant, and saloon.

"I had not enough to pay those extravagant bills. Lucretia loved champagne, Pete, and her parents were fond of oysters and brandy. But, as fortune would have it, the cook of the trail driver had died from drinking too much bad whiskey in one of Saint Jo's lesser establishments, and my new friends pleaded with the trail boss to hire me. The trail boss, a Captain Yarborough, had a fine reputation with the citizens of Saint Jo, so they agreed that I could go to Kansas, where Captain Yarborough would see that I wired them the money the Corbett & Dougherty Traveling Troupe owed.''

''And did you?''

''Of course not. We were not a mile out of town when Captain Yarborough informed me that I had a job as long as I could drive a team and fill a coffee pot with something drinkable and a stew pot with something tired drovers might consider grub. He also told me that if I sent Saint Jo one dime, he would personally blow my head off. Those swine had killed his cook, and he said he would never do business in that town again.

''So, to conclude a rather long story, I found that I could drive a team, and also that I could cook quite well. I've been at it ever since. Your supper's getting cold, Pete. Now are you sure you don't want any sonnets?''

''Thanks, but no, J. W.''

''Then I leave you with this, from Henry Ward Beecher: 'Flowers are the sweetest things that God ever made, and forgot to put a soul into.' Oh, blast it, my cigar's out.''

Julian Cale let the animals and men rest just outside of Fort Griffin. First, he sent J. W. Dougherty and Hannah into town to buy supplies. When they returned later that morning, Pete and Buddy were gone.

"Mr. Cale is letting us go into town two at a time," Chris informed her. "Figures there's less chance of us getting into trouble that way. And he advanced us all a whole five dollars. Ain't that something?"

"Don't say ain't."

"Yes ma'am. I forgot. Well, Paul and I are going in as soon as Pete and Buddy get back. I'm gonna buy me a hot bath and a shave, and then find some sarsaparilla and maybe an ice cream parlor."

Hannah smiled. Chris had a few more years before he would ever need a razor and he'd be hard-pressed to find an ice cream parlor in town. He could use a bath, though.

"Mr. Cale had planned to send that Dunson fellow in with Buddy, but Pete asked to go first, so Mr. Cale let him. Boy, Andy Dunson sure had a burr under his saddle after that. First, he cussed Pete up and down. Well, Pete was gone by then. Then he cussed Mr. Cale, with Mr. Cale right there. Dunson said five dollars wouldn't buy nothing in Fort Griffin and he had a lot more money coming to him. Mr. Cale, he says that he's only advancing five bucks, and if Dunson don't like that he could take his horse and go to . . . well, you know. Dunson finally cooled off after Cal Maddox said he'd buy the first round at the Bee Hive Saloon and they'd tree the town as much as five dollars a piece would allow."

"No fights?"

"No ma'am. Just a lot of cussin'."

"Well, I have just the cure for those ill tempers," J. W. Dougherty said. "Peach pie for supper, and for you and Master Richmond . . ." he pulled out two pieces of candy.

"Thank you!" Chris's face brightened and he took the peppermint sticks and ran to find Paul.

"You're a sweetheart, Mr. Dougherty," Hannah said. She pushed back her hat and wondered why Pete was in such a hurry to go to town.

They called the village that sprung up near Fort Griffin "The Flat." collection of saloons, brothels, shanties, and beer gardens—plus a handful of respectable businesses—had attracted buffalo hunters before they killed most of the buffalo, soldiers from the garrison up on Government Hill before the Army pulled out and cowboys heading north to Kansas. Gunmen such as Pat Garrett, Dave Rudabaugh, Wyatt Earp, Doc Holliday and Bat Masterson had sampled The Flat's wares. The sound of banjos, fiddles, and player pianos seldom stopped. Too often gunfire accompanied the music.

That's what Pete had been told to expect at Fort Griffin.

"If I didn't know no better, I'd say this was just some prayer meetin' camp," Buddy Pecos commented, sending a river of tobacco juice onto a boardwalk in front of a saloon. On the building's facade, painted in glittery gold, read the words:

THE GET-DRUNK SALOON

Just below, nailed to the warped doors, was another sign:

OUT OF BUSINESS

An old man with teeth the color of Buddy's boots weaved his way down the creaking boardwalk, leaned on the hitching post in front of the saloon, and asked, "You gents on a trail drive?"

"Yup," Pecos answered. "Town's changed."

The man grunted something. "Yes sir," he said. "Yankees abandoned the fort five years ago this month. Ain't been many herds this year. Got a school now, the Fort Griffin Academy, passel of churches, and some stores. Bunch of Baptists calling on the sinners to get on the righteous road. But if you gents got sinning in mind, you can still get the job done. I should know."

"How 'bout a place to wet our windpipes?" Pecos asked.

"Best place is still the Bee Hive," the old-timer replied.

"How about some flowers?" Pete asked.

"What?"

Pecos and the old man spoke the words in unison. Pete could see the puzzled expression on the old-timer's face and feel Pecos's one eye boring through

with a "What the Sam Hill are you talkin' about?"
glare.

"Flowers," Pete repeated. "Roses, daisies, those
kinds of things."

"Flowers!" The man shook his head and scratched
his chin. "Bluebonnets is all burned up from the heat.
I never heard tell of no one buying no flowers in The
Flat." He turned and staggered down the boardwalk.

Pete turned to face Pecos.

"I hope," his friend said, "you'll let us cut the dust
before we go huntin' flowers."

"Place is abuzz with activity," Pecos said as they
entered the Bee Hive, and he cackled at his own joke.
Pete laughed too. Buddy seldom made jokes.

They carved a path through the thick smoke, tables
and two men picking banjos and singing *You Naughty,
Naughty Men,* and leaned against the bar. "Two ryes
and two beers," Pecos said, and the bartender stopped
twisting his greasy mustache and nodded.

"Thanks," Pete said.

"What for? Them's mine."

Pecos wasn't joking, so Pete ordered a beer. They
took their drinks to an empty table in a corner. Belissari
fanned tobacco smoke with his hat. Pecos chased down
his first rye with his first beer and wiped the foam from
his whiskers, satisfied.

"You serious 'bout them flowers?"

Pete shrugged. "I figured finding flowers to be long
odds, but maybe some chocolates or a book of
Dickens."

"If I were you, I'd just challenge Maddox. Call him out. You're a fair hand with a gun."

"The key word, Buddy, is 'fair.' Cal Maddox could be more than fair."

"He ain't. I'm an excellent judge of gunmen. I'd bet on you, pard. 'Course, your gun could misfire. That Remington you bought is bulky, balance ain't as good as a Colt. And I prefer my Schofield. But cowboys ain't much good when it comes to serious gunplay. They like to advertise leather and gun shops with their wardrobe, but facin' a man down, nah. Now—"

"Buddy. We're not having this conversation. I'm not drunk. You're not drunk—yet, I think. I'm not getting into a gunfight with Cal Maddox."

"Well, maybe not no gunfight, but you're gonna have to fight him. And—"

Both men looked up. A woman stared down at them. A shawl covered her outfit of red satin and netting, and she must have applied the rouge on her face with a trowel. Her carrot-colored hair was damp with sweat, and when she spoke, she revealed crooked teeth, bad gums, and breath that could kill a grizzly.

"Which one of you's lookin' for flowers?" she asked.

Chapter Eleven

The string of picket cribs lay across the dark alley behind The Get Drunk Saloon. The redhead opened the door to the third hardscrabble building, and Pete nervously followed her inside. Carrot Top lit a lantern and sat on the edge of the rusty iron bed. There wasn't much room for anything else in the crib. A wash stand rested on a chair in the corner, and dirty laundry had been thrown over another chair. Two small windows were open, not that they were needed. The gaps between the wooden pickets wouldn't keep out snow or rain, let alone a nice breeze.

"Make yourself comfortable, sugar," Carrot Top said.

Pete cleared his throat. He had left Buddy back at the Bee Hive, nursing on his third round of drinks.

Now he wished he had brought the sharpshooter with him. "The roses," he said.

Laughing, the woman stood, put a bony finger against her left nostril, stuck her head out the nearest window, and blew her nose. She fell across the bed on her belly and began rooting on the floor away from Belissari. After a minute, she sat back up, a bottle of liquor in her left hand and three red roses in her right. A broken whiskey bottle served as the vase.

She tossed Pete the liquor. He caught it with his good hand, his back to the open door, and looked at the flowers. They needed water.

"The mayor's wife grows them things," the woman said. "I helped myself to 'em the other night. Thought they might add a little color to the joint. You got a head cold?"

Pete pushed his hat back. The rawhide stampede string caught underneath his Adam's apple and reminded him of how dry his throat felt.

"That's better," Carrot Top said. "Have a drink, sugar. I don't bite." Pete wasn't so sure.

The redhead waited. Pete finally relented, withdrew the cork, and took a sip. He wanted to wipe the bottle first, but didn't want to insult the woman, prostitute or not, at least when she had a few roses to sell. The rotgut tasted like carbolic acid. Pete coughed. The woman laughed.

"Sugar, let's get down to business. You want to buy them roses?"

"Yes, ma'am." He could barely talk. The liquor had burned his throat.

"Fifteen dollars, and they're all yours."

Belissari relaxed, and had another sip. The rotgut didn't taste quite as bad now, and Pete felt more in his element. He was haggling, like trading for a horse.

"A dollar," he countered, thought for a second, and added: "For the whole lot. You can keep the vase."

"Honey, now I got to make a livin', and all you seem interested is in my roses. So you're costin' me good money. Fourteen dollars."

"One-fifty. My partner and I already bought you two whiskeys at the Bee Hive before you brought me over."

"Tasty liquor too, it was. But, handsome, I have to pay for this place. Eight dollars a week. And rent's due day after tomorrow."

You're being cheated, Belissari thought. This place wasn't worth being chopped up for kindling. "A dollar a rose," Pete said, knowing his price was way too high. His head swam. He wanted to get out of here now. "That's three dollars—for stolen merchandise too, I'll add. Take it or leave it."

Carrot Top sighed. She looked up at him and smiled. "Let's drink on it," she said. "But toss me the money first."

"What do you mean Pete's in jail? Bud-dy!"

Hannah put her hands on her hips and waited for Buddy Pecos to reply. The gunman closed his red-rimmed eye and grimaced at Hannah's shouts. He rubbed both temples as J. W. Dougherty placed a tin cup in front of him. "Coffee and castor oil, Buddy," the cook said. "She'll fix you right up or put you down quicker than a .45."

Hannah glared some more. Buddy sipped the concoction and looked up.

"Well!"

Pecos swallowed. "He went to see this crib girl to—"

"A crib girl!"

"What's a crib girl, Uncle Julian?" Paul Richmond asked.

"You're too young," Dougherty answered, forcing back a smile.

Hannah kicked a mound of dust over Pecos's boots. Buddy fell back, spilling the dark drink over his chaps. He righted himself as Hannah demanded, "What do you mean a crib girl?"

"Well, he was lookin' for flowers, and this gal comes sashayin' into the Bee Hive." Pecos stopped suddenly, swallowed, and stuck his head between his knees. The wave of nausea passed, and Pecos looked up, three shades paler than he was before.

"Go on," Hannah said.

"So we buy her a few drinks, and she offers to sell Pete some flowers. Roses, I think. Pete looks at me. I kinda shrug. He decides to check it out. He goes off with her. I stay in the Bee Hive and have a few more drinks. Next thing I know, the bouncer in the Bee Hive has tossed me out and said for me and my saddle-bum pals to keep out, and I see the deputy marshal dragging

Pete feetfirst to the calaboose. Deputy says Pete was bustin' up all the cribs, screamin' something about Medusa, some garden with nymphs and a dragon with a hundred heads.''

"Muy loco," the elder Mendietta whispered, crossing himself.

"Getting his mythology mixed up is all,'' Dougherty commented.

Hannah blinked. "What did Pete say?''

"Nothin'. He was out deader than dirt. Deputy said he was lockin' Pete up for disturbin' the peace and messin' up the cribs. Said we could bail him out if we wanna.''

Andy Dunson swore. "Bail him out. Let's break him out.''

"You don't even like Pete, Andy,'' Cal Maddox said.

"I know. But it would give us something to do. Shoot the town up. Add a little excitement.''

"All right, settle down.'' Julian Cale had finally spoken. "Hannah, you want me to get Pete out of jail?''

"I'll take care of Pete Belissari,'' she said.

Pete pushed the slop bucket away and climbed back into the narrow bunk. It was like scaling Mitre Peak. Someone opened the door and a thousand footsteps echoed through the narrow hallway between the cells. His eyes opened. A somber, bespectacled gent in a gray sack suit and five-point star frowned at him. Beside him stood Hannah, looking more like the goddess Tauris than Aphrodite, matched the marshal's frown.

"How do you feel this morning?" the marshal asked.

"Horrible" came a barely audible reply.

"So you don't want to cut off Medusa's head and stick it in a goatskin bag, aren't afraid of being turned into stone, aren't looking for The Garden of the Hesperides and aren't trying to slay a dragon with a hundred heads?"

Belissari blinked. "I said that?"

"That's what my deputy got out of you before he had to plant the butt of his Spiller and Burr against your head? This lady wants to get you out of jail, but I'd like to hear your story, son, without the Greek mythology."

"I'd like to hear the story too," Hannah said.

Pete searched his mind. He had been trying to take three golden apples from the garden of the four daughters of Night who kept The Garden of the Hesperides when the dragon attacked. He wasn't sure where Medusa came from. Fog lifted from his mind. Reality hit.

"I was trying to buy some flowers," he said. His eyes met Hannah's stare. "For you." A wave of nausea forced him to seek out the slop bucket again.

"You want some coffee, son?" the marshal asked.

"No," Pete answered and sat on the cot again.

"A crib girl told me she had some roses for sale. I can't recall where she said she got them. I went to see for myself. We haggled over a price. That's all I remember."

"What did this girl look like?"

Pete shook his head. She had snakes instead of hair, and a hideous face. Scales covered her body, and her tongue was forked like a serpent's. No, that was Medusa. "Red hair," he said, remembering. "Ugly as sin."

The marshal smiled. "That would be Wichita Wendy. She never was known to water down her whiskey with water, so you're not the first gent she drugged. Deputy saw her getting on the midnight stage to Jacksboro last night. Town Council has been wanting me to run her out of town, and all the other crib girls, for some time. You done me a favor, son. Now, how much did it cost you?"

Pete managed to stand without toppling over. He searched his pockets. His watch was missing, and his money, not that he had carried much. So was his Remington, gun belt, and Barlow knife. He informed the lawman.

"I've got your revolver and leather in my desk. Wendy must have taken your knife, watch, and money. She never did care much for firearms. And the deputy said Wendy had some flowers in her hair when she left. Roses, I think. I guess she got those too. I reckon we can let you go as soon as you pay a fine."

Hannah spoke. "He gets fined for being drugged and robbed?"

The marshal shrugged. "Well, he was disturbing the peace, miss. Could have hurt someone. Resisted arrest. And I get a percentage of all the fines I collect. Ten dollars or twenty days."

Hannah paid the fine, helped Pete find his horse, and the two rode back to the cow camp in silence. Pete slid from the saddle and crashed to the dry earth.

"Well," Julian Cale said, "I figured that I could trust you and Buddy to act like men, not a bunch of dumb waddies, buy yourselves a bath and a couple of drinks in town, then come on in and let some others have a little fun. But both of you come back looking like you've been slopping hogs for a month. You get arrested. Buddy gets the rest of us banned from buying a whiskey at the Bee Hive, and here it is a day later and nobody else has been to town."

He worked on his tobacco for a few seconds, spit juice into the fire, and continued. "I'd be all for pulling out, but likely I'd be lynched on the spot if no one else got to see The Flat because of you. My deal stands. Two men in town at a time, but you have two and a half hours only. Longer than that, and I come to bring you back. And nobody's going be happy with that. Chito and Dunson." Cale checked his timepiece. "You get your carcasses back here by twelve-thirty." The two cowhands ran to the remuda, their spurs and laughter sounding like music. Cale spit again. "Belissari," he said. "You get back on your horse and get to the herd with your sorry partner. That hot sun will do you some good. That's an order."

Faustino had brought the horse back. Pete gingerly made his way, took the reins, and leaned against the horse. He knew he was being challenged, knew Cale didn't think he could stay in the saddle for a minute, knew every hand in camp, and Hannah, expected him to fail. Belissari tried to bring his foot to the stirrup but couldn't. He held his breath, thinking his stomach might not cooperate. The sick feeling subsided. Pete tried again. He made it to the stirrup but couldn't pull himself into the saddle. No one spoke, but he felt their eyes locked on his back. Another feeble attempt caused someone to snort.

Finally, Belissari led the horse to the chuck wagon. He stepped up on the wagon tongue, inhaled deeply, and half-jumped, half-fell into the saddle. The horse stutterstepped, but Belissari controlled the reins, gave the animal a couple of kicks, and rode to the herd.

"That was pathetic," Cal Maddox said, more to Hannah than anyone else.

Watching Pete, Hannah walked away from Cal Maddox. "Pathetic?" she said to herself. "Not by a long shot." That was Pete, the old Pete, stubborn . . .

Chapter Twelve

Two days later, Pete had worked Wichita Wendy's poison out of his system. He still couldn't saddle his own horse—with one arm in a sling, he had a hard enough time just getting mounted—but the pounding had left his head, J. W. Dougherty's grub didn't go down like live earthworms anymore, and the cowhands were teasing him about his trip to The Flat. He even laughed himself.

All of the other cowboys had returned from town in decent shape, although Andy Dunson sported a black eye and Texas-size hangover, and Paul and Chris came back disappointed that ice cream couldn't be found in Fort Griffin and shocked over the price of sarsaparillas.

The broken country south of the Red River stretched before them, but Pete couldn't see a thing but brown dust that burned his eyes. He heard the ''yip-yip-yip'' and ''hi-yah'' of his comrades riding drag, urging the longhorns along. Comrades? Faustino, Paul, and Chris? Pete had thirteen years on the oldest of the bunch. When Pete tried to join in with a ''Keep-a-moving, keep-a-moving,'' all he managed to do was bite into his dirty bandanna. He spit out the cloth, frowned at the taste, and wet his cracked lips with his tongue.

By the will of Zeus, he said to himself, *this is my last cattle drive.*

His legs felt numb when he dismounted that afternoon. After stamping his feet to get the blood flowing again, he walked to the chuck wagon for some of Dougherty's bacon, biscuits, and coffee while Irwin Sawyer roped and saddled a fresh horse.

''How's the view from the south?'' Buddy Pecos asked.

Pete smiled wearily. ''Better than looking at your sorry face.''

Pecos laughed, emptied the dregs, and tossed his coffee cup into the wreck pan. ''We'll make a top hand of you yet, pard,'' the old sharpshooter said and made a bowlegged trek to the remuda.

Pete washed down his meal with strong coffee and sought out Hannah. Hatless, she sat on the gate of the hoodlum wagon, her back to him, eating her meal. Alone. Cal Maddox must be back with the herd, he thought. Then again, even Maddox had kept his distance from Hannah recently. She had hardened herself for this cattle drive. She had to. Pete realized this now, but he had even seen her crack a smile the other night when the hands teased him about his rose-buying excursion.

If they talked, if he let her know everything would be fine, he might be able to patch up a few pieces. He walked toward her.

"Hey, Pete."

Belissari turned. Chris—at least, it resembled Chris underneath that dirt and grime—pointed a fork toward the north. The boy swallowed a mouthful of floury biscuit and asked, "You ever seen a cloud like that? What is it?"

Pete spun around. He spotted the burnished white wall against a brilliant blue sky, maybe a mile from where the longhorns grazed. Belissari blinked. The cloud moved with the wind. Beto Mendietta rose from his perch on the chuck wagon's tongue and stared. So did Paul Richmond and J. W. Dougherty. The others in camp, including Hannah, hadn't noticed the unearthly haze.

"That's not a cloud," Pete said softly. His mind flashed back to the St. Elias the Prophet Greek Orthodox Church in Corpus Christi when he was twelve or thirteen and the Very Reverend Father Athanasios Manuel reading from the Old Testament. Leviticus, he thought. Or was it Deuteronomy?

Thou shalt carry much seed out into the field, and shalt gather but little in; for the locust shall consume it.

Pete had already turned and thrown his cup at the wreck pan when Julian Cale rode into camp at a high lope and jerked his bay to a sliding stop.

"Every man in the saddle and to the herd! *Now!*" Cale screamed.

Hannah spilled coffee on her skirt as she leaped from her seat. The brilliant white cloud obscured the sun. The ground began to shake, and she realized the herd was stampeding. Again. She could tell now though that the longhorns were running away from camp, so she had nothing to fear from the cattle.

But this?

The color of the flying, moving wall changed to brown. It was almost upon them now as J. W. Dougherty called her name. She turned.

"Get under the wagon," the cook said. "Cover your head. Don't worry. They'll be gone soon."

"What is it?" she asked.

Dougherty's answer was lost in a deafening roar from the sky. Hannah twisted to see a swarm of insects covering the blackjacks and grass, blotting out everything. She ducked underneath the hoodlum wagon as grasshoppers thumped against the wood. Burying her face in her hands, she shook as the locusts covered her, feeling them crawl over her clothes and hair, trying to breathe in hot air, afraid to open her mouth or even move.

The shrill din of the grasshoppers petrified her, a thousand years from the pleasant chirping of cicadas in the summer. Stampedes she could handle. Renegade outlaws, Apache, flash floods and even drought. But this? This was unnatural, a scourge of Egypt sent by a vengeful Old Testament god.

She felt the drumming of the locusts' sheer wings, the prickly sensation of their legs as they crawled about her clothes and into her hair. Hannah moved now, swatting at the insects, violently brushing her hair, then shaking her head savagely as she crawled underneath the wagon, crushing grasshoppers with her hands and knees. She stumbled suddenly, clipped the side of a wheel with her head, and fell hard on the locust-covered ground. Blood trickled down her head, and she felt the grasshoppers cover her blouse.

Sighing, she succumbed to the plague and fell into a welcomed state of unconsciousness.

"Hannah?"

Her eyes opened. The cacophony of the grasshoppers was gone, and J. W. Dougherty knelt over her, gingerly applying a wet bandanna against her cut head. Slowly she sat up. Her skin crawled, and she looked down, expecting to find locusts covering her, but most of them were gone, and none covered her clothes.

"Oh, my," she said, looking down at her blouse.

The pillow ticking shirt had been ivory with green stripes, but the grasshoppers had devoured the stripes so that the blouse now hung about her in threads. She pulled the useless garment off, and brushed a dead insect off the front of her camisole.

"I'll get you one of my shirts," Dougherty said, embarrassed, and sprinted to the wagons.

She heard something clicking behind her and untied her black scarf. She shook out the piece of silk and saw a locust fly away, revealing an uneven hole in the bandanna. Sighing, Hannah looked around. Grass had been consumed, branches of trees stripped. Drought had already given the land a worn appearance, but now the whole countryside looked like dead winter. She saw another white cloud in the distance and felt herself shivering momentarily before realizing that the new cloud was only thick, blowing dust.

"Here you go, Hannah."

She took Dougherty's blue calico shirt and pulled it over, retied the ruined bandanna and walked to the hoodlum wagon where she found her hat, shook off a few grasshoppers, and sat down wearily.

"You ever seen anything like that?" she asked.

Dougherty nodded. "Ten years, no, probably a dozen years ago in Kansas. Stripped corn down to the cob, cabbage, everything in only a hour or so. How's your head?"

She touched the cut with her fingers. "I'm all right," she said and scanned the country around her once more. The swarm of insects had cut a swath through an already scorched land. Before her lay desolation, and she was looking north, the direction the herd had to move.

"How much trouble are we in, J. W.?"

The cook frowned. "I'm not sure," he replied.

"What happened to your head?" Pete asked her.

She shook her head, mumbled a "nothing, just bumped it," and excused herself. Julian Cale was motioning for her to join him and Beto Mendietta by the chuck box.

Pete sighed as she walked away and accepted a cup of coffee from Pecos.

"That's about the runningnest bunch of longhorns I ever laid eyes on," he said. "We're lucky we ain't had a man or hoss killed yet."

Belissari grunted a reply and headed to the remuda. He didn't feel much like talking.

"You two got a pretty big interest in this herd," Cale told Hannah. "I represent me and the other ranchers who put their fate in my hands. Anyway, we got a choice to make, and I figured we'd best put it to a vote." He paused to carve off a healthy bite of tobacco with his pocketknife.

Hannah and Mendietta glanced at each other and waited. Cale put the chew in his mouth and worked the tobacco to a comfortable position before continuing.

"This drive ain't going worth a spit, folks," he said. "We've lost more cattle than I care to count in stampedes, and now this. It's like God's cursing us." He spit. "So we got a choice to make."

She waited. Mendietta nodded at Cale, and the rancher wiped his mouth with the back of his hand.

"I sent Cadwallader east and Ruthven west to find

out how much grass them pests ate," Cale continued. "I rode a few miles north after we got the herd settled down, and, well, it don't look good."

"What are you saying?" Hannah asked.

"I'm not sure we can get these cattle to Kansas." Cale swore. "To tell the truth, I'm not even sure we can get them out of Texas. Them longhorns are worn out, and if there's nothing to eat, well . . ."

Mendietta nodded solemnly, whispering, *"No es bueno."*

"What are our options, Mr. Cale?" Hannah said. "We can't go back to Fort Davis."

Cale frowned. "I know a rancher west of here on the North Pease. We might be able to sell our herd to him, cut our losses, not lose everything."

Hannah was already shaking her head before Cale finished. "If the locusts stripped his grasslands too, he'd be in worst shape than we are," she argued. "He couldn't take on more cattle. And even if the locusts missed his land, he'd be a fool to buy a herd in the middle of a drought with the range like it is."

Mendietta nodded in agreement.

Cale spit. "You're right. I didn't say it was an agreeable option, but it's there. We can also try to drive the herd east, to the railhead in Denison, find a buyer there maybe. But we'd probably have to lease land to graze the cattle, and we might have to stay a good while just to fatten them up to fetch a decent price."

The three fell silent for a minute, considering the options. Hannah didn't like the idea of driving to Denison, didn't like Cale's use of "decent price." A grazing lease would cut into the profits substantially, especially if they had to wait a month or two before selling the herd. She had heard stories from old cowboys about grazing cattle all winter just waiting for a boost in the market. And she knew cattle fetched better prices in Dodge City than Denison. But could they make it to Dogde City?

"And if we go on?" Hannah said. "To Kansas?"

Cale shrugged. "Could be that north of the Red wasn't hit by the grasshoppers," he said and spit again. "Could be otherwise too. We'll have a better idea at Doan's Crossing, but just getting the herd to Doan's will be difficult. And if we make it there and find the grass in the Nations is gone, then we're going to be shooting a lot of starving cattle."

"So it's a gamble either way," Hannah said.

Julian Cale almost smiled. She would have sworn to it. "That's what the cattle business is, Miss Scott," he said. The old rancher exhaled. "Those are the options, folks. I reckon it's time to vote. Hannah?"

Her mind had been set a long time ago. "Dodge City," she said.

Cale nodded and turned to Mendietta.

"Con permiso," the old Mexican said. "Dodge City."

"Reckon my vote don't matter," Cale said. "We'll head north."

Chapter Thirteen

Sitting in the saddle on his lean dapple, Sergeant Major Cadwallader shook out a loop and tossed the lariat at Belissari's feet. The horseman grabbed the rope with his good hand and awkwardly fastened it over the dead bull's massive horns. When he had finished, Pete nodded at Cadwallader, who backed his horse up a few steps so the noose fastened.

"How many does that make?" Cadwallader asked.

"I haven't been counting," Pete answered.

Cadwallader turned his horse and dragged the dead carcass away. Shielding his eyes from the dust, Belissari slowly walked to Poseidon. When he could see, he sadly watched the mulberry longhorn being pulled unceremoniously to a dry wash to be dumped with a dozen or more other dead cattle. Ruthven and Pecos

115

had butchered one animal for food, but the rest of the meat would go to waste. And Cale wouldn't spend precious time skinning the dead cattle to salvage their hides. The quicker they got out of this wasteland, the better. So J. W. Dougherty would pour coal oil over the animals, piled with wood, and burn them in a makeshift funeral pyre.

What a waste, Pete thought. Even that stubborn son of Satan deserved better. He dreaded the ride back to camp.

"El Moro's dead."

Hannah's blue eyes were cold, almost hollow. She stared at Pete blankly and nodded. "I know," she said. "Cal told me."

"I'm sorry."

Pete swallowed. He thought he might cry himself when he discovered the old bull, dead from exhaustion or starvation, or maybe he just plain gave up. He remembered branding the crazy, mean-spirited bull when Hannah first bought him, recalled how El Moro had treed him in a juniper weeks back, weeks that now seemed like years. He swore to himself. That old bull had seemed invincible, a Hercules on hooves.

"You all right?" Pete asked.

Hannah swore sharply, so unexpected that Pete took a few steps back. "Come on, Pete," she snapped. "It was just a bull."

Pete watched dumbfounded as she stormed away. Surprise turned into anger. He looked down at his sling and saw he had clenched his fist—and it hadn't even hurt.

She sat alone, massaging her temples, wondering if God had cursed her for her sins. She slapped her hat against her skirt, filling the air around her with dust, and wiped the dirt off her dry, leathery hands. Biting her lip, she steeled herself against the sorrow.

El Moro was a bull, a range animal, just as she had told Pete. It wasn't like he was a pet. He was mean too. You don't cry over dead bulls. *But did I kill him?*

She looked ahead at the worthless earth that stretched before them. Julian Cale said they were another day from the Red River. The cattle and horses could drink their fill of muddy water there. But would they be able to graze? Maybe they should have tried for Denison.

"Have some water, Hannah," Cal Maddox said and handed her the canteen.

Hannah thought about declining, but dust caked her throat, and she was desperately thirsty. She greedily drank the warm water and thanked the curly-headed cowboy.

"Cal," she said, and stopped.

Maddox took the canteen from her hands and threw the strap over his shoulder, sloshing water on the front of his chaps.

"Hannah," he said, "you don't have to say a thing. Everything's gonna be fine. I know it don't look too promisin' right now, I know you're upset about El

Moro—so am I, he was a good lead bull. But I've been in tighter spots. We'll be dancing a jig together, drinking champagne in the Long Branch and laughing about all this in a little bit. Just you wait and see.''

He left her with a smile. She let his words sink in, and, for now, believed him. They could tough this out. There would be grass in the Indian Territory. She frowned suddenly, wishing Pete had spoken those words instead of Cal. Sadly she realized she hadn't given Pete the chance.

Cadwallader let out a grating Johnny Reb cry, pretty good for an old buffalo soldier, and galloped into the camp, leaping from the saddle before his horse had stopped.

''Grass, my friends!'' he shouted, his white teeth glistening underneath cracked, bleeding lips. ''Leaves on trees. It's heaven, boys.'' He looked at Hannah and swept his hat off his head. ''And you too, Miss Hannah.''

Pecos shook his head. ''You're dreamin', Sergeant. Out of your head.''

Cadwallader reached inside his vest and withdrew a tiny branch from an oak, its leaves green and fresh. ''Well,'' he said, ''I know this isn't exactly the garden of Eden, but I'll take it.''

''How far?'' Cale asked.

''A mile. No more.''

Hannah joined in as the trail hands let out a cheer that would have caused a stampede if the animals weren't half-dead.

They let the cattle and horses graze near Doan's Crossing for two days, while the trail crew relaxed in the shade, played cards at the Bat Cave dugout, and passed the time with Corwin Doan in his adobe store or anyone else who'd listen. Hannah decided to take a bath at McBride's Hotel until she realized how much it would cost. She went to the Red instead. The river was shallow, muddy as usual, but she managed to wash enough off the grime so that she felt respectable at least.

Cale checked for mail, but Doan, who had served as the postmaster since '79, had nothing for him. The two haggled over the price of supplies, finally agreed, and loaded the chuck wagon with flour, beans, and canned tomatoes.

The following morning, they crossed the Red River and into the Indian Nations.

"I don't like Indians," Andy Dunson announced after they had bedded down the herd.

Chito Ruthven laughed. "You don't like nobody, Andy."

And nobody likes you, Pete thought. They had been in the Nations for a few days, but had yet to see any Indians. This lay west of Kiowa, Comanche and Apache territory, but Julian Cale half-expected some brave to ride out and parlay for beef, maybe charge a toll to cross their land.

Dunson was arguing against having anything to do with Indians, not that his opinion mattered.

"Indians are useless," Dunson droned on. "Why, if I saw one now—"

A scream silenced him. Looking at the blackjack stand, Pete pulled himself up, reached across his body until his left hand rested on the Remington's walnut butt—and quickly let go. He'd blow his leg off trying to shoot left-handed.

Dunson cursed and pulled his own revolver. "That's probably a Cheyenne Dog Soldier."

"Shut up," Pete barked. They were too far south for Cheyenne, and that scream had come from no Indian warrior. It sounded more like a boy's. *Christ!* Heavy footfalls sounded in the woods and Paul Richmond raced from the trees holding his left arm tightly.

Pete was running toward Paul when the teen half-fell into Buddy Pecos's arms. "S-s-s-s-snake!" Paul cried.

Pecos threw the boy on the ground and shouted. "Be still!" But Richmond squirmed on the ground, crying, choking out, "It bit me! I'm gonna die!"

Pete was by them now, and he sat on the boy's chest, pinning Paul's arms down as he kicked and screamed. Pete echoed Buddy's order to be still and looked down at Richmond's left arm, already swollen, with black fang marks centered four inches from the boy's wrist.

Pecos unsheathed his massive bowie knife, and when Paul saw the blade, his eyes froze and he stopped fighting Belissari's grip. The kid screamed, however, when Pecos made quick incisions over the bite and bent his head, sucking and spitting venom and blood as quickly as he could, taking time only to wipe his mouth quickly before repeating the process.

Paul's lips trembled. He looked up at Pete and cried, "It bit me. It was a rattler. I'm gonna die."

"You're not going to die, Paul," Pete said and smiled. He wanted to keep Paul's attention, make him relax, keep the venom from spreading rapidly. Buddy finished trying to suck the poison and wrapped chewing tobacco over the wound to draw out more venom. "Buddy," Pete said lightly. "You ever known a body to die of snakebite?"

Pecos concentrated on tightening his bandanna over the boy's arm. "Nope," he said. "I ain't. How 'bout you?"

Belissari shook his head. "Not in Texas. Now, back in ancient times, Poseidon sent some serpents down to strangle Laocoon and his two sons. That—"

"Your . . . horse," the boy said between sobs. "Poseidon . . . did that."

Pete laughed. "No, Paul. The Greek god Poseidon. My horse is scared of snakes."

The trail crew had gathered around them now. A couple laughed with Belissari and Pecos. Pete felt his own heart slow down. Paul breathed rapidly and his eyes showed fear, but he seemed to be settling down.

Julian Cale's restrained words hovered in the air. "You just toughen it up, lad."

Pete felt the old rancher towering behind them as Pecos finished his doctoring. Paul stared at his uncle for a few seconds, faced Belissari again, and asked in a shaky voice, "Am I gonna die?"

Pete shook his head. "You'll have more girls chasing you than you can shake a stick at, wanting to see that scar and have you tell them all about how you wrestled a rattler in the middle of Indian Territory."

The boy smiled weakly. "I'll have a scar?"

"I expect so. What do you think, Buddy?"

"Maybe so," the Texan said. "How many rattles did that snake have, Paulie?"

"I didn't count!" he exclaimed.

Buddy and Pete clucked their tongues. "Next time," Pete said, "do a better job. Count the rattles, skin the snake, and then come to camp and let Buddy kiss your arm."

Paul laughed. Pete was aware of J. W. Dougherty kneeling beside them, a bottle of whiskey in his right hand. "Lift his head," the cook said, and Pete complied. Dougherty uncorked the bottle and made Paul take a healthy swig. The boy immediately went into a coughing fit, spraying Pete, Dougherty and Pecos with whiskey.

"You've been holdin' out of us, J. W.," Pecos said.

Dougherty ignored him. "Get him to the wagon," he said.

With one arm, Pete couldn't lift the boy, so he stood up and let Pecos handle the chore. His eyes met Hannah's briefly, but then she was following Buddy and Dougherty. Pete inhaled deeply and slowly exhaled. His wrist hurt again. He knew he was sweating. He looked up to see Chris, face drained of all color and eyes filled with tears, staring at him. "Will Paul be all right?" the boy asked.

"You bet," Belissari answered, surprising himself. He put his left hand on Chris's shoulder, squeezing it gently, and listened as the cowhands patted Paul as if he were a war hero, their voices singing out.

"Thataway to shut up Andy Dunson, Paul. I'll buy you a whiskey in Dodge."

"Glad you didn't bring that snake back. Dougherty woulda made us eat him for supper."

"I bet it wasn't even a rattler. You know how Buddy likes to cut on people with that bowie."

Pete and Chris smiled at each other and followed the parade.

Chapter Fourteen

They buried Paul Nathaniel Richmond shortly after sunrise. Hannah stood behind Chris, her hands on his shoulders, listening to him sob as J. W. Dougherty read from the Book of Matthew and the Mendiettas waited by the canvas-wrapped body, holding their hats, ready to lower the teenager into a shallow grave for all of eternity.

Cattle lowed in the distance, and the wind rustled through the trees. Hannah felt a tear roll down her cheek and wanted to brush it away but couldn't let go of Chris. Young Paul deserved better. He should have a fine coffin instead of a wagon tarp, with a choir singing in a church. He should have roses instead of cheap grass and a brilliant marble tombstone instead of the poorly made wooden cross that would blow over with the first strong wind. No, she thought. That's not right at all. Paul Richmond didn't deserve any of this. He didn't deserve to die.

Dougherty finished the Beatitudes and closed his bible. "You want to say anything, Mr. Cale?" he asked.

The rancher shook his head and stared at his dead nephew. "No," he finally spoke. "Y'all best get the herd up."

The cowhands turned and walked away, silently putting on their hats, moving to the remuda. Chris followed them and stopped in front of Pete. The boy wiped his eyes and swallowed.

"Y'all was joking with him," he said. "I thought he'd be all right."

Pete's head dropped. He clenched his fist, rolling up the brim of his hat. "I know," he said softly and looked up. "We—" He sighed.

"It ain't your fault," Chris said and walked away.

Hannah stared at Pete. At first she wanted to scream at Pete, then she wanted to console him, tell him that she understood they had been trying to calm Paul to keep the blood from spreading the rattlesnake's venom. She also wanted to bury her head against his chest, but she had vowed she wouldn't cry on this drive, and she didn't count the stray tear at the funeral. It wasn't Pete's fault, or Buddy's, that Paul died. People reacted differently to snakebite. One wiry cowhand back in Fort Davis had been bitten seventeen times by rattlers and had never even gotten sick. His arms and legs were pockmarked beyond belief—that's what the cowboys said; she had never seen them, but . . .

If it's anyone's fault, she thought, *it's mine.*

She turned back to the grave. Beto and Faustino shoveled sand over the lowered body while Julian Cale silently watched. Hannah closed her eyes and prayed. She heard Pete's footsteps as he joined the hands by the remuda. When her eyes opened, the Mendiettas were walking past her, heads bowed, carrying their spades. Alone, Julian Cale still stared at the grave.

A solemn mood shrouded the camp for the next few weeks. Julian Cale seldom spoke, and J. W. Dougherty's flirtations and quotations all but ceased. Three steers drowned at the Canadian River. Hannah wondered if any would be alive by the time they crossed into Kansas.

The country flattened before them. Hannah half-heartedly flipped the reins to keep the wagon moving. Her stomach informed her that it must be nearing suppertime, and she looked west to see the sun beginning to dip below a barren horizon that stretched endlessly. The sky shined a brilliant blue in the west, as well as east and south. But to the northwest, the way they were moving, hung a wicked black cloud.

Dougherty pulled up alongside her in the chuck wagon and pointed his chin at the cloud. "You see that?" he shouted above the jingling of traces and squeaking of wheels.

"Yes. We're headed right for it."

"And it's heading straight for us."

They had wanted rain for months, but this cloud

threatened more. It moved as a testament of power, daring anything to challenge it. She knew the herd would stampede again.

"What do we do?" she asked.

"Find a safe place."

"What about everyone—"

"They'll have to take care of themselves, and the herd." He pulled ahead of her and she followed, parking the wagon beside his in a dip in the ground, too small for a flash flood but low enough to offer some protection from an already strong wind.

Thunder crashed, and the chuck wagon's tarp popped in the wind. Lightning split a black sky that turned late afternoon to midnight. Dougherty wrapped a slicker over her, and they crouched in the hollow. The cook was saying something now, but Hannah couldn't tell if it was Shakespeare, Poe, or Dryden. A cold wind numbed her face. Suddenly she understood that J. W. Dougherty wasn't reciting a monologue—he was praying.

The cattle ran at the report of a thunderbolt, but Pete didn't chase after them. He couldn't. His horse, a piebald gelding not worth the time spent shoeing him, spun in a circle as the wind blew the rain sideways in hard, icy sheets.

Lightning struck nearby, and the storm roared furiously. Piebald continued to spin and snort, and Pete knew he'd never stay in the saddle for long. Not with one good hand. Not in this tempest. He freed his feet from the stirrups and leaped from the saddle, slipping in the wet grass but managing not to fall on his right arm. Quickly he rose. His horse was gone. The rain blinded him, and the wind almost blew him down. He bent forward and moved slowly, swaying until he struck something hard. A tree.

Belissari grabbed a branch and held on. This wasn't smart, he told himself, knowing lightning could strike this tree and fry him like bacon, but Belissari couldn't let go. It was a sturdy oak, though even it creaked and groaned in the wind, but it seemed the closest haven he'd ever find in the storm. He slid to a seat, resting his back against the tree's trunk, holding onto the branch with his good hand.

The wind droned on. He felt cold and waterlogged. Thunder rolled while seconds stretched into minutes. A verse of *The Iliad* flashed through his mind:

> *The man does better who runs from*
> *disaster than he who is caught by it.*

Pete Belissari laughed. "I should have run away," he said aloud, "about two months ago."

His drenched hat tightened like rawhide on his head the next afternoon as he made his way north, trying to find the herd. The storm had passed within an hour, though it had been followed by a few friendlier showers, but by then night had fallen, and Pete decided it would be best to spend the night underneath his friend the oak tree. At dawn, he sloshed his way southeast, hoping Piebald would have run with the wind and found a place to hide.

Thank you, Apollo, he said to himself two hours later when he saw the gelding in an overflowing creek bed, drinking water and splashing the water playfully. The pinto didn't even try to run when Pete approached him, tightened the saddle cinch, and struggled into the saddle.

He smelled Dougherty's coffee and let the aroma guide him to the camp. Pete dropped to the earth and saw Hannah and Dougherty kneeling by a crumpled figure on the wet earth. Pecos, Chris, and Maddox stood over them, not speaking. Absently Pete dropped the reins and moved forward.

"We 'bout given you up for dead," Pecos said quietly.

"Not yet," Pete said and knelt beside the battered figure of Julian Cale.

"Hold him, Hannah," Dougherty said. Pete grimaced, watching Cale's face tighten in pain as Dougherty set the broken leg with a hard jerk. Hannah leaned forward and wiped blood from the old rancher's lips and asked Pecos to fetch Dougherty's whiskey bottle.

"How is he?" Pete asked.

Hannah looked up. "Bad," she said. "We think his horse rolled over on him, but we didn't find him until late this morning. Lift his head."

Pete gently pulled Cale up as Buddy squatted beside them with the liquor. The rancher's eyes opened and he took a small sip, sighed, and mumbled a soft curse. Pete lowered the rancher's head onto a saddle being used as a pillow.

Cale's eyes fluttered and finally focused on Belissari and Pecos.

"Seems like every time I join up with you boys, I water a lot of ground with my blood," he said hoarsely and broke into a coughing fit. His breathing was ragged, and he spit out a froth of blood.

"Well," Cale whispered. "I got my nephew killed. Now I got myself killed."

"You're not going to die, Mr. Cale," Hannah told him.

"Yeah. We'll see," he said and drifted into unconsciousness.

Hannah said something. Pete slowly realized she had called his name. He looked into her eyes. "Pete," she said. "We have to get him to a doctor or he's going to die."

Belissari nodded. "Buddy," he said, "how well do you know this country?"

"Fair to middlin'. Been a spell since I've ridden these parts."

"We're near Fort Supply, right?"

"Yeah. It's north of here."

Cal Maddox cleared his throat. "The Springer Ranch is southwest, might be a hair closer than the fort. But how do we get him there?"

"Hoodlum wagon," Pete said. His eyes landed on Chris. "You think you and Hannah can get—"

Julian Cale woke up with a cough. "You boys ain't buried me yet," he said and managed to laugh.

Pete smoothed his mustache and scratched his bearded chin, thinking. "Julian," he said, "you need a doctor. We're going to put you in the hoodlum wagon and take you to Fort Supply or the Springer Ranch."

"I'm not going to Fort Supply and have some Yankee sawbones work on me," Cale blurted out. "Springer Ranch is in Texas. I'll go there."

"Mr. Cale, the fort will have a doctor," Hannah pleaded.

"The Springers can fetch one from Mobeetie. I'm still the boss of this outfit, and I'm going to Texas."

Pete nodded. Maddox said, "Ranch's easier to find. Right off the Canadian on this side of the river."

"All right," Belissari continued. "Hannah and Chris will—"

"Hannah stays put." Cale coughed again. "The boy can get me there all right, and we can't spare any more men. Besides, I'll need Hannah to haggle for a good price for our beeves once you get them to Dodge. Where's the rest of the boys?"

"With the herd," Pecos answered.

"Good."

Belissari couldn't help laughing. Julian Cale was as stubborn as . . . Hannah. Pete relaxed. Julian was too mean, too ornery to die.

The rancher coughed again. "All right, that's settled. The boy will drive me to the Springers—watch them bumps, Chris, or you'll rue the day—and you get that herd moving. You're burning daylight. Hannah will handle the money in Dodge.''

Dougherty, Pecos, and Maddox lifted Cale carefully and put him in the back of the hoodlum wagon. Chris and Pete moved all of the tack, war bags, and soogans into the chuck wagon, while Hannah covered Cale with a bedroll and tried to make him comfortable. As Dougherty and Pecos hitched the team, Maddox gave Chris instructions on finding the Springer ranch. The teen climbed started to climb to his seat, but Hannah hugged him tightly and kissed his cheek.

''Mama Hannah!'' Chris said, embarrassed, maybe disgusted.

''Be careful,'' she said.

Shaking his head, Chris climbed into the seat and released the brake.

''Wait a minute,'' Cale ordered. ''Belissari.''

Pete leaned over the side of the wagon and stared at the pale rancher. ''I need to leave somebody in charge,'' Cale said. Pete nodded, expecting Pecos or even Dougherty.

''You're the trail boss, Belissari.''

Pete's mouth fell open. Cale must be joking. ''Julian,'' he said, ''I'm no trail boss. I'm not even a decent cowhand.''

''You get things done, son. Now get this done.''

Chapter Fifteen

Pete expected his election to go over about as well as Lincoln's did in the South.

It was worse.

"You can't tell the workin' end of a longhorn from a jackrabbit, and I'm supposed to be takin' orders from you?" Dunson shook his head. "That don't make a lick of sense."

Belissari sat on the tongue of the chuck wagon, flexing his right wrist. He had removed the sling and kept testing his arm. Stiff? Yes. Sore? Plenty. But he had movement. He tried picking up his coffee cup. No problem. He sipped some as Dunson's tirade continued.

He expected Andy to be against the promotion. Dunson took a stand against anything and everyone. Cal

Maddox had voiced his displeasure, though not as loud as Dunson; Chito Ruthven grunted something and swore underneath his breath; and Irwin Sawyer rolled his eyes. The Mendiettas stood by silently. So did Pecos and Cadwallader. Pete knew he could count on Buddy and the Sergeant Major—inside, they were probably laughing at this—and the Mendiettas. And Dougherty? Well, even the good cook might terminate the friendship once Pete told him what he had in mind. For now, though, he just let Dunson spew his venom.

"This drive has reached trail's end," Dunson said. "That's all I gotta say."

"I wish," Pete whispered, as the cowboy continued. "Ol' Cale must have been delirious when he left you in charge. We're supposed to listen to you just because that ramrod says so. He's probably dead by now. I just ain't about to take no orders from some horse-lovin' greenhorn who knows books but nothin' else."

"Then draw your time, Dunson," Pete said, and slowly rose.

That quieted the cowhand. He stared at Pete dumbfounded. "You don't mean that," Dunson said.

"I do. You take orders from me, or you ride out— with a promissory note. We pay off in Dodge City."

Dunson snorted. "How you gonna get the herd to Dodge without me?"

Belissari laughed. "We're not in some awful fix. We'll ease the herd to Fort Supply, and I'll hire one or two cowhands at the sutler's store. We're going on to Kansas, mister, with or without you."

The cowboy tugged on his mustache, thinking. That took some effort.

"Well . . ." Dunson paused. "How you plan on movin' the herd to the fort? The Richmond kid's dead, the other boy's gone with Cale. We're short-handed, and them cattle's all worn out. You gonna let the Mendietta boy ride drag all by his lonesome?"

Pete let Dunson finish. Since Richmond's death, Pete, Faustino, and Chris had been alone on drag. Chris was gone, and Pete would have to scout out water holes and campgrounds. One rider couldn't handle the drag by himself. Dunson was right about that, but with the herd as tired as it was, two could do the job—at least to Fort Supply.

"No," he answered. "Dougherty will help him out."

"Me?" The cook bust out laughing.

Belissari smiled, turning to the actor/cook. "What was it you told me, J. W.? A cook in his life plays many parts? It's time for a new role, *o fi'los mou*. Hannah can drive the chuck wagon. She can cook too. And it's only to Fort Supply . . . maybe."

Was it time for a speech? Might as well get it over with. Pete emptied his coffee cup and tossed it to the wreck pan. He briefly stared at his right hand. The motion hadn't hurt. Clearing his throat, he stood by the fire and spoke:

"Listen, I didn't ask for this. I didn't want it. I could say no, and put Buddy in charge. Or *Señor* Mendietta. But Cale was right about one thing. I can get things done. That's because I'm as mule-headed as''—he almost said Hannah but stopped himself—''one of those though longhorns out there. Now we can stand around here all week and argue about it, but that won't get this herd to market. Or we can forget about it and just do our jobs. We'll try to hire help at Fort Supply, but if we can't, well, that's our bad luck. Trial crews have been short-handed before. If we lost all of our horses, we could walk to Kansas.'' That was a lie. Pete wouldn't walk anywhere. Nor would many cowboys. ''So that's the story. Anybody who wants to quit, I'll write you a note. You can see me in Dodge City to collect. We'll be wetting our windpipes at Lightner's.''

Oops. Lightner's was in Fort Davis. Pete didn't know any saloons in Dodge City, but no one noticed. He sat down beside Cadwallader and Pecos. Dunson shook his head but said nothing. Dougherty stared in disbelief, maybe shock, but finally grinned and went back to stirring his pot of stew. Pete felt embarrassed. He didn't like making speeches.

''Nice stumping, Mr. Belissari,'' Cadwallader said. ''Let me know when you run for governor. I might vote for you.''

''I won't,'' Pecos said, trying hard to smile.

Fort Supply lay on a sandy bottom near the junction of the North Canadian and Wolf Creek. Most southwestern military forts were open enclosures, but this one had two blockhouses and a high, wooden palisade wall, surrounded by canvas tents, a couple of corrals, and shoddy parasite structures.

A squad of soldiers, looking hot and bored, marched around the compound as a sergeant barked orders.

"Make you homesick?" Pete asked.

"Not hardly," Cadwallader replied.

Belissari spotted the sutler's store, a half dugout on the west side of the post, and rode toward it. They left the herd grazing a few miles south, and Pete brought Cadwallader along, figuring the soldier's presence would help him at the fort. Pete reined Poseidon to a stop and dismounted, wrapping the reins around the rickety hitching post in front of the store. A fat man in a dirty apron and railroad cap of red wool appeared at the door, sipping from a small bottle. The label read "Dr. J. H. McClean's Volcanic Oil Liniment," but Pete figured something else was in the bottle.

"What can I do for you gents?" Fatty asked.

Belissari wiped sweat off his forehead and replaced his hat. "Got a trail herd south of here and we're short of men. We were hoping to find some here."

"Headin' to Dodge?"

"Yes, sir."

Fatty drained his bottle and tossed it on top of a trash pile beside the dugout. "Man would be a fool to leave the comforts of Fort Supply to push a bunch of Texas beef all the way to Dodge." He made it sound as if Dodge were a thousand miles away. To hear Buddy and Maddox, they only had two more weeks on the trail.

"You don't know of anyone looking for work?"

"Nope. Now, some dumb waddie might happen

along, though, in a day or so. If I was you, I'd let my beeves graze and bring your crew in here. Play some cards. Fight some bluebellies. Y'all could have a right smart of a time.''

Pete glanced at Cadwallader and shook his head. ''I guess not,'' he said and turned to go.

Fatty cleared his throat. ''Well, you boys should come in and cut the dust,'' he pleaded.

''No thanks,'' Pete said, and mounted Poseidon. Fatty disappeared inside the store. Pete urged the mustang a few paces and waited on Cadwallader.

''Well?'' Belissari asked.

The soldier shrugged. ''I could ask one of those troopers to desert.''

A man grunted behind them. ''I might know somebody who could help.''

Both men turned in their saddles. Beside the trash pile stood a tall man, grinning like a schoolgirl, wearing a buckskin shirt and kersey blue trousers. He was olive-skinned with flowing black hair—a full-blood Comanche brave.

''You hired a savage for a cattle drive?'' Cal Maddox shook his head.

''Niet-tomo is far from savage,'' Pete said. ''He's a friend of mine.'' Belissari glanced over his shoulder to make sure the Indian hadn't heard Maddox. Niet-tomo—Winter Wind in English—sat by the chuck wagon, drinking coffee and carrying on with Hannah as if they were long-lost siblings. The Comanche was showing Hannah his note, the one he had handed Pete back at Fort Supply.

To whom it may concern:
This is Niet-tomo, a friendly Comanche. You may call him Winter Wind. He has a good grasp of the English language and a strong desire to see more of our world. Please grant him any kindness. He will not harm you. He must return to Anadarko by 1 September 1886.
Perry Anderson
Agent, Anadarko, Indian Ty.

Two years ago, Pete had barely beaten Winter Wind in a horse race, and a few months later, the Indian brave and two friends helped Pete, Buddy, and Julian Cale rescue Hannah from a renegade outlaw.

"We have a hundred miles to go. Winter Wind can do the job."

Maddox stubbornly shook his head. "An Indian can't drive cattle."

"Con permiso," Beto Mendietta said and fired off a Spanish reply while his son nodded in agreement. Maddox stared blankly at the Mexicans before turning to Belissari.

"I don't savvy that lingo," he said.

Pete smiled. "He says he is sorry to disagree with you but he lost enough cattle over the years to Apache and Comanche that they must know something."

Buddy Pecos lit a cigarette. "Beto's right, Cal. And

I've heard you say it before, Cal: 'Cowboy don't need no brains; it's the hoss that counts.' Besides, Pete's right. We only got a little piece to go.''

"Yeah, well, I'm sleepin' with my Colt. I don't fancy wakin' up scalped."

Pete swore. "Think, Maddox! There hasn't been any trouble with the Comanche in years. Winter Wind won't bother you, or anyone else, and nobody is going to harm him. He has permission to leave the reservation—the agent thinks it's good for him to see more of the white man's ways—as long as he's back by the first of September, and that's not a problem. He's going with us to Dodge."

The cowboy shook his head and walked away. The Mendiettas left, and Pecos squatted to finish his cigarette. Pete refilled his coffee cup and sighed, exasperated. J. W. Dougherty laughed.

'' 'Unbidden guests are often welcomest when they are gone,' '' the cook-now-cowhand said.

Pete sighed. *"Et tu, Brute?"*

Dougherty laughed and handed Belissari a cigar. "Not at all, my friend. I welcome the chance to perform in front of a Comanche, to teach him to appreciate fine literature and finer acting."

"Well, you'll have plenty of time and opportunity since the two of you will be riding drag."

The cook's smile flipped into a hard frown.

Sand Creek was dry north of Fort Supply, but they found some water at the North Fork of Buffalo Creek.

Pete discovered that he actually liked the job of trail boss. He got to ride Poseidon out each morning, ahead of the herd, scouting territory he had never seen. It wasn't much to look at, compared to the Davis Mountains, and an unceasing wind chapped his lips and left his long hair in knots. But it definitely beat riding drag.

Winter Wind, on the other hand, had the makings of a pretty good cowhand. Even Maddox had warmed up to the Comanche, and J. W. Dougherty loved the attention the Indian gave him during his nightly readings of Shakespeare.

Four days after leaving Fort Supply, the herd swam the Cimarron River and camped that night in Kansas.

The crew relaxed. Pete took his plate of bacon and beans and cup of coffee from Hannah and sat beside Pecos and Cadwallader to eat his supper.

"You boys noticed how much better things have gone since Pete started bossin' us?" Chito Ruthven asked. "Boys, we shoulda turned Old Man Cale loose months ago and made Pete captain then. Woulda been a tad easier on us."

"Yeah," Cadwallader said, "but then Pete wouldn't have gotten to ride drag. And we all know how much he loves that."

An explosion of laughter rocked the camp. Pete chewed on a piece of bacon and smiled. Behind him, he heard Hannah's giggles. This felt good.

Ten days later, they bedded down the herd on the banks of the Arkansas River. Pete, Hannah, and Pecos rode into town with Winter Wind, who wanted to see

Dodge City. Thick black smoke poured into the sky, and a train whistle blew as they fought the traffic on Front Street. In the center of the street, a hand-painted sign, now well faded, read:

THE CARRYING OF

FIREARMS STRICTLY

PROHIBITED

VIOLATORS PAY A $100 FINE

And below that:

TRY

PRICKLY ASH

BITTERS

Welcome to civilization, Pete thought.

A weather flag flapped in the breeze on top of a brand-new brick building on Front Street. R. M. WRIGHT & CO. read the sign, and an urchin stood at the corner hawking newspapers. Pete reined up, pulled a coin from his vest pocket, and tossed it at the boy's feet. The kid handed him a paper. Pete looked at the *Dodge City Times.*

"What's the big news?" Pecos asked.

"It's Thursday, August nineteenth," Pete said. Having lost all track of time, he bought the paper just to know what day it was.

Hannah laughed. "So, Winter Wind, what do you think of Dodge City?" she asked.

The Comanche nodded appreciatively. "I think," he said, "You all owe me fourteen dollars."

Chapter Sixteen

The expression on the bartender's face soured when Hannah entered the Varieties. The barman stopped polishing a glass and stepped back, folding his arms and dribbling his fingers against the black garters high on his white shirtsleeves. Hannah was sure he would have thrown her out of the saloon, with pleasure, if Buddy Pecos hadn't followed her inside.

Undeterred, Hannah walked to the empty bar and looked down the long building. Several men sat at tables that lined the papered walls, their faces clouded by cigar smoke. A few stood talking at the far end of the saloon, while a dirty boy, probably not even in his teens, gathered the brass spittoons for cleaning.

Hannah faced the bartender. His frown hardened, but he unfolded his arms and pulled on the ends of his thick, black mustache. "Mr. Wright says I might find a Raymond Coburn here, from the Chicago Packing Company," Hannah said. "Could you point him out?"

The bartender twisted his mustache and placed the clean glass on a shelf behind him. He didn't turn around.

Buddy Pecos cleared his throat. "You got a hearin' problem, buck?"

When the bartender faced them again, his face had paled considerably. He quickly looked away from Pecos's scarred, leathery face and nodded at Hannah. "First table on the left, sitting alone."

Hannah left without thanking the man. The table sat under one of the tall windows and below a lamp hanging from the wooden ceiling. She was glad of that. Both provided a bright spot in an otherwise dark building, though she could see serpentine gray smoke drifting through the rays of sunlight. Raymond Coburn looked up, sat a tumbler of whiskey in front of him, and slightly rose, tipping his gray high derby, introducing himself and sliding back into his seat. Hannah wondered if most cattle buyers drummed up much business drinking alone in a saloon south of Dodge's notorious deadline, where firearms—and everything else—were allowed and encouraged. Then again, to hear Mr. Wright talk, the cattle business had all but played out in Dodge City.

Wearing a dark sack suit and narrow necktie, Coburn was a man of average height and appearance, with blue eyes, slick brown hair and a mustache and long goatee beginning to gray. Hannah accidentally kicked his carpetbag under the table when she and Buddy sat down.

Hannah introduced herself and Buddy. Coburn nodded politely. Pecos suggested a drink. Coburn agreed, but seemed awkward and confused when Pecos left him alone with a woman.

She tried smiling. It didn't work, so she went straight to business. ''I'm representing a mixed herd from the Davis Mountains in Texas. Understand you, or your company, is in the market for some prime Texas beef.''

Coburn forced a smile, nodded, and looked toward the bar. Pecos was taking his time, sampling a cigar before bringing the whiskeys to the table.

''Mr. Coburn?''

He turned back to her and cleared his throat. ''Yes, Mrs.—''

''Miss.''

''Yes, Miss Scott. How many head do you have?''

''About twenty-four hundred.'' She thought about that sadly. They had lost two hundred during the drive.

Coburn glanced at the bar. He sighed. Buddy still hadn't brought those drinks. ''I'd have to see them, of course, before I can made a decision. What price are you looking at?''

''I'd like fifty dollars a head,'' she said, ''but I don't think you'd go for that.'' She smiled, letting him know she was kidding. The cattle buyer only looked confused, maybe even scared, before his face finally relaxed.

Pecos sat down and slid a tumbler of whiskey across

the table. Coburn held up the glass in a salute and took a healthy swig. He smacked his lips, relieved.

"We were getting down to discussing the price of your cattle, Mr. Pecos," he said.

Buddy shook his head. "Her cattle, amigo. She's the boss."

Coburn frowned again. He drained the rest of his whiskey and put the empty tumbler down heavily. Slowly, unsurely, he looked back at Hannah.

"Mr. Coburn," she said, "Mr. Wright spoke very highly of you, sir, and we'd like to give you first crack at buying our cattle."

"That's why I'm in Dodge City, Mrs. . . . Miss Scott."

"Good. We're camped on this side of the river, just east of town. I've got some hands who would like to be paid off, and I'd like to find a hotel, buy some clean clothes, and take a hot bath." Coburn's face turned red. Hannah let his embarrassment pass. Pecos slid him his half-empty glass of whiskey, which the buyer readily accepted and shot down like lemonade.

"Perhaps you'd like to look over our cattle tomorrow morning, and we can haggle over a price?"

Coburn blinked. "Haggle?"

"Haggle, Mr. Coburn. But mind you, I want your highest price."

She rose. "Tomorrow morning?"

He nodded in confirmation, and she and Pecos left the Varieties.

"Thirty-one fifty a head. Mr. Coburn, you've got yourself a deal."

Raymond Coburn sighed heavily with relief. He briefly scribbled on his notepad, chewed on the end of the pencil, and said, "My men put the count at two thousand three hundred and eighty nine." Beto Mendietta, who has also tallied the herd, nodded at Hannah in confirmation. "That brings our price to . . ." He started scratching out the math equation.

"Seventy-five thousand," Hannah said, "two hundred and fifty-three dollars and fifty cents." She had already done her own ciphering.

Coburn looked up, amazed. "That's correct," he said. "Shall we meet at the bank on Monday morning? I'll have the papers all in order."

"Yes. But can you advance us some money so I can pay off the crew?"

With a nod, Coburn opened his carpetbag and withdrew a billfold thick with cash. He counted out twelve hundred-dollar bills and handed them to Hannah, then made her sign a receipt. "Nine o'clock Monday, Miss Scott?"

Hannah nodded, and Raymond Coburn hurriedly left the camp.

"He'll probably resign next week," Cal Maddox told her. "I bet he'll never do business with a woman again."

"Can't blame him," Dougherty said, grinning.

Pete stayed with Beto Mendietta, who had no desire to see Dodge City, and Winter Wind, who had seen enough, to watch the herd while the rest of the crew, including Hannah, rode to town that Saturday morning. They changed Coburn's hundreds at the bank, and Hannah handed each cowhand his pay in smaller bills. She paid them off in full, though she was sorely tempted to hold back ten dollars for each man, just so they wouldn't leave Dodge City flat broke.

Chito Ruthven cut loose with a Rebel hoop and yelled, "The first round's on me, boys! Last one to the Comique is a pumpkin roller!" With a flying mount, he spurred his bay at a high lope down Front Street, almost causing two wagons to wreck and pitching one rider to the dust with a thud and a curse.

Cal Maddox took his pay last. He slipped off his head, and bowed slightly after sliding the folded bills into his vest. "I promised you we'd cut a jig at the Long Branch and laugh at them hard times," he said. "Remember?"

Hannah smiled. "Some other time, Cal. You go have some fun."

"Hey, Maddox!" Dunson called from his saddle. "Come on, pard. I wanna discuss a business proposition with you."

"I'll catch up with you, Andy!" Maddox said without looking.

Cal and Hannah stood on the boardwalk. Slowly the cowboy put on his hat and scraped his boot heels against the wooden planks. "Well, I reckon I can at least keep you company, Hannah. Stop any ruffians from tryin' to make your acquaintance."

"Cal," she said softly, "I'm going to shop and check into a hotel and catch up on three months' sleep. You go find a pretty girl—"

"I've already found one."

"The wrong one, Cal. Go on. I'll be fine."

The cowboy frowned. "Well," he finally said, "at least I can escort you to the Centennial Barber Shop. I'm gonna get my locks shorn, then spend some of this money. But I ain't lettin' you out of that dance, Hannah Scott."

She let him take her arm, and they strolled down the crowded boardwalk until Cal stopped and said good-bye in front of a business advertising "Haircutting done in the latest fashion." After he disappeared inside, Hannah felt her own dirty, unkempt hair. She suddenly felt like—what was her name?—Calamity Jane, but no one seemed to notice. After a brief tour around McCarty's drugstore, she returned to Wright's brick building and loaded up on a pair of women's longjohns (for the winter), a nightgown (for now), undergarments, and a blue prairie dress of soft cotton. She also found some *MuGuffey's Readers* (for the children), a two-pound can of Blanke's Mojav Coffee (a present for Winter Wind), soap, shampoo, and a stick of peppermint candy (for herself).

Bags in hand, she checked into Bisland's Hotel, a two-story frame structure on Front Street near the railroad station, asked for a hot bath immediately, and went upstairs. A half-hour later, she lay soaking in the clawfoot tub, wearing only her St. Christopher medallion, chewing the last bit of her peppermint stick, and wondering if she had ever felt better. She waited until the water turned icy before climbing out, leaving about twenty pounds of trail dirt in the tub. She brushed her clean hair, put on her new nightgown, and fell onto the comfortable mattress, half-expecting to fall asleep immediately. It took her a long time, however. The bed was too soft, and she kept staring at the walls and the ceiling. After more than three months herding cattle, sleeping under the stars and on hard ground, being indoors seemed eerie.

Hannah awoke hours later to the clamor of an ear-splitting bell and the shouts of men outside her Room 231 window. With a yawn, she sat up and rubbed her eyes, wishing they would quit with that racket below. City noise, she thought with disgust. After disrobing, she pulled on her new petticoat and reached for the blue dress when she realized something was wrong.

The commotion outside continued. Hannah tried to open the window, but it was painted shut. She peered out, but her view was of an empty alley and the wooden side of the neighboring building, with BARNES & WILSON'S MEAT MARKET written in large block letters of fading yellow paint. The disturbance came from Front Street, in front of the hotel. Still, she made out figures carrying buckets and splashing the wooden walls of the Meat Market.

"Oh, my," she said. The market must be on fire. She froze, catching the scent of thick black smoke. Clutching the St. Christopher medal, she ran across the room, leaned against the door, and slowly cracked it open. She stepped outside in her underwear and gasped as orange-white flames licked the wall in front of the stairway. Hannah spun around. Her mouth hung open. That way was blocked too, as the roof came crashing down twenty feet away in a maelstrom of smothering smoke and chunks of burning wood. Stifling heat drove her back inside, and she slammed the door shut. She pulled her hair, trying to think, and leaned back. The door was hot now, and she moved away, turning to see smoke pouring through the cracks and hearing the crackling of timbers consumed by fire.

Chapter Seventeen

Gasping for air, Hannah struggled to open the window. With no time to waste, she looked around the room for something to break the glass. A ceramic pitcher sat on top of a chest of drawers. She grabbed it, but with shaking hands dropped it and cringed as it burst on the floor. The heat intensified. Water, she thought, and submerged herself briefly in the tub of dirty bathwater. That would help, but not for long.

She climbed out of the tub and grabbed a chair, raising it over her head as she ran toward the window, her one avenue of escape. The door exploded, and she felt a blast of heat envelop her as she stumbled to the floor. Her lungs burned with each ragged breath, and she coughed as the room filled with thick, sickening smoke. Hannah rolled over, covering her mouth and nose, trying to find air as she crawled desperately to the window.

Glass shattered. She looked up but couldn't see. Her eyes burned. Strong hands pulled her off the floor and buried her face against a strong chest. "Hang on," a voice said. The man stifled a cough. "Put your arms around my neck and don't let go."

"Pete?" she asked wearily.

"Cal," Maddox said, lifting her like a child into his arms.

Glass bit into her left leg as Maddox crawled out the window. A rope hanging from the roof swayed in the breeze through the alley.

"Hey!" someone shouted from below. "Look up there!"

Maddox gripped the rope with both hands. "Don't let go," he repeated. "Hang on tight."

She tried to swallow.

With Hannah clinging to the cowboy, Maddox dropped from the windowsill. His boots slammed into the wooden wall of the hotel and he bounced away, sliding down the rope a few inches and bouncing into the wall again. Hannah jerked with him. She looked up to see flames surging out of the window above, searing the rope as they snaked their way to safety.

"Cal?" She choked. They dropped a few more inches.

The rope snapped.

Hannah landed feetfirst in the dirt with a jarring impact that snapped her head back. She crashed to the ground, and Maddox fell on top of her, sending the precious little air in her lungs out with a whoosh. Cal rolled off her and scooped her into her arms, carrying her across the street and laying her gently on the boardwalk.

Her eyes flickered, and with Cal's help, she slowly sat up, coughing hard, leaning against the cowboy's shoulder and watching a red pump-wagon spray the flaming Bisland Hotel with water while firemen in their bib-front shirts scurried around with shovels, axes, buckets, and orders. Other volunteers, men and women, had formed a bucket brigade and drenched the neighboring buildings, valiantly trying to save those structures while the Bisland burned out of control. It was futile. Flames were already spreading across the roof of the Meat Market and another building.

Her ribs hurt. She had bitten her tongue, her eyes burned with pain, and she still couldn't get enough air. Hannah slid down, resting her head on the boardwalk, and tried to tell herself this was only a bad dream.

Pete galloped past the smoldering ruins near the railroad station. It looked like the whole block was gone. He whipped Poseidon down the street toward the two-story frame building where a crowd had gathered underneath the awnings, gaping inside the tall windows. In almost one movement, he leaped from the saddle and wrapped the reins around a wooden column.

"Hey, you can't leave that horse there!" a man called out, but Pete ignored him, pushed through the rabble, and raced inside the Great Western Hotel.

"Where is she?" he shouted.

J. W. Dougherty put a firm hand on Pete's shoulder. "Easy," he said. "The doc's with her now in the office. She wasn't burned any, but she inhaled a lot of smoke." The cook released his grip. Pete waited until his heart slowed, took a deep breath, and sat down on an oak parlor sofa beside Pecos and Sawyer. In front of him, newspaper reporters surrounded Cal Maddox, peppering him with questions and praise. A waiter brought the cowhand a glass of whiskey and asked if he could shake Cal's hand. The waddie smiled and obliged, then sipped his whiskey as a reporter said, "You realize, Mr. Maddox, that in addition to saving that young woman's life, you probably also kept this city from burning to the ground. How does it feel to be a hero?"

Pete didn't care to hear the answer. He gave Pecos a hard stare. "What happened?" he asked.

Buddy shrugged. "I was doin' my drinkin' south of the deadline, pard. Way I hear it, Cal spotted the fire at the Bisland Hotel, was first to sound the alarm, then climbed on top of the market next door, lassoed the hotel chimney, and went crashing through a second-story window and dragged Hannah out of the room. Pretty handy."

Sawyer grunted. "Town almost burned to the ground last year. If Maddox hadn't seen the fire when he did, the whole town mighta gone up in smoke, and Hannah with it. I reckon Maddox would get a lot of votes if he was to run for mayor here."

Belissari leaned back in the sofa, took one quick glance at Maddox, and looked away, leaning forward, resting his arms on his knees, smoothing his mustache. Someone—he thought it was Dougherty—asked if he needed something from the bar. Belissari shook his head and closed his eyes tightly for a few minutes, trembling in a strange mix of anger and relief. He sat up sharply.

"How did the fire start?"

Pecos said, "No idea."

"What was Maddox doing here?"

It was Sawyer's turn to shake his head. "I seen him and Dunson drinkin' at the Varieties. Reckon he left. Maybe he was lookin' for Hannah."

A thousand questions flashed through Pete's mind. How did Maddox get there so fast? How did he know Hannah was in that hotel? How did he see her? How did he . . ."

"Whoa, pard," Pecos said. "I know what you're thinkin'. But don't you go makin' accusations yet. Look at him. Cal Maddox is a hero in this town. And you're forgettin' one important fact."

"What's that?"

"He saved Hannah's life."

The door behind the front desk opened, and a middle-aged man with a weak chin and silver spectacles emerged from the office. The room fell silent as the doctor closed the door and walked to the center of the room. "Which one of you is Maddox?" he asked.

Cal stepped forward. "I am," he said, handing his empty glass to a friendly reporter.

"She'd like to see you," the doctor said, putting on his hat. "Don't stay long, though. She needs her rest."

Maddox's long legs carried him quickly across the floor. Smiling, the doctor turned to the crowd and said, "I think she'll be fine. She's a strong woman."

"Can we talk to her?" a reporter asked.

"No, not now. Maybe tomorrow."

The newspapermen surrounded the doctor, firing off questions about Hannah. Pete stared across the room at the door Maddox had closed behind him.

"You weren't tryin' to get out of that dance by dyin' on me?" Cal Maddox asked. "Were you?"

Hannah smiled and motioned for Cal to sit down on the oak rocking chair by the bed lounge where she lay. The mattress wasn't comfortable, but the doctor had informed her the Great Western planned to move her into their best suite later that day, at no expense too.

Maddox removed his hat, rifling his fingers through his curly hair. Cal rocked awkwardly, his jingling spurs keeping time as the chair squeaked. "How you feel?" he asked.

"Hurts to breathe."

"That'll pass. Doc says you ate a lot of smoke."

"I think you broke some ribs when you fell on me."

Cal frowned. "Uh," he said, "I, uh, well . . ."

"I'm joking, Cal."

"Oh. Good. I'd never want to hurt you, Hannah." He stopped rocking and reached forward, covering her right hand with his, squeezing it gently.

"Cal," Hannah said, "I just wanted to thank you for saving my life."

"Shucks, Hannah," he said. "I just happened along. Coulda been anybody. And you was almost to the window when I come crashin' through. I bet you woulda made it out by yourself anyhow."

"And probably broken my neck."

Cal shook his head. "No, ma'am. Just a leg mor'n likely."

Hannah laughed, and regretted it. Her chest ached. "Would that," she asked, "have gotten me out of that dance?"

"Not likely. I'd dance with you on crutches."

"Thank you, anyway, Cal."

"No need. Besides, it ain't every day I get to see a pretty woman in nothin' but her petti—" He sat up straight, dragging his spurs across the wood. "I'm sorry. There I go talkin' without thinkin'."

"It's all right."

He relaxed. "Well, does that mean I have to marry you now?"

"I don't think so."

"Too bad."

She swallowed and frowned, remembering. "Ohhhh, all of those presents I bought. They must have burned."

"Along with half a block of town," he said. "Don't fret none, Hannah. The bank didn't burn, and you got seventy-five thousand dollars waitin' for you there. That'll buy a lot of presents."

"It's not all my money, Cal."

She closed her eyes, tired all of a sudden. Cal leaned over and kissed her forehead gently, then rose and donned his hat. "You rest, Hannah. I'll see you later." He started to open the door as Hannah called out: "Cal, would you send Pete in for a minute?"

Maddox turned around, silent for half a minute. She looked at him. "He, well, Pete ain't here, Hannah. He's still with the herd."

"Oh." She felt her heart break.

"I can send for him if you'd like."

"No," she said. "That's all right."

Chapter Eighteen

Pete saw Hannah the next day in her second-story suite at the Great Western Hotel, after J. W. Dougherty and Raymond Coburn and a gaggle of reporters and slew of town businessmen and churchwomen had paid their respects. He and Hannah talked briefly about nothing important, though Pete really wanted to question her about the fire. Buddy Pecos was right. He had no proof, and Hannah was alive.

That Monday morning, with Hannah still resting in her room, Pete met Coburn at the bank and handled the final details of the cattle transaction. Belissari opened a temporary account at the bank and bought a canvas satchel at a mercantile between G. M. Hoover's cigar store and the tonsorial. He carried the satchel to Hannah's room. She was asleep, so he left it by her bedside. Next, Belissari and Beto Mendietta went over the remuda, choosing the horses they would keep. Afterward, he and the Mendiettas drove the rest to the livery stable on the west end of town, where Pete and the owner debated for forty minutes before agreeing on a price. Pete put that cash to Hannah's satchel.

"You seem to be taking to this cattleman's job," Hannah told him.

They smiled at each other. She was in better spirits, partly because of the money but mainly because of the telegram he had brought her that afternoon:

MADE IT TO SPRINGER STOP MOBEETIE DOC
SAYS MR CALE IMPROVING STOP MISS YOU
STOP CHRIS

Pete left the hotel and walked down Front Street. He bought a new shirt and book at Wright's, and went next door to the Long Branch. He ordered a beer and drank half of it immediately. Someone called his name. Belissari turned and faced a weaving Andy Dunson.

"Well, horse drover, you got your money and got your . . ." He lost his train of thought. "You got everything but your woman."

Belissari hit him then, crushing Dunson's nose with the beer mug. He followed through with a hard left into the cowboy's stomach, dropped the smashed glass, and slammed a right into the temple. Dunson dropped in a bloody heap, and Pete started to kick the unconscious man's face but felt himself being jerked away and slammed against the long mahogany bar.

"He's had it, mister!"

Pete came up hard, ready to fight, but stopped. His chest heaved as he stared at the unfriendly faces of a bouncer the size of a longhorn bull and a man in black broadcloth who came through the batwing doors, slapping a long, black cane and wearing a shiny star.

"What's going on here?" the lawman asked.

"Nothing," the bouncer said. "The drunk on the floor insulted this gent. It's all over, Marshal."

"Good." The lawman's steel-gray eyes fastened on Belissari. "Do your drinking, friend, south of the deadline. Lou, drag that drunk's carcass out back with the dogs." He stared at Pete again. "Mister," he said evenly, "when I said do your drinking south of the deadline, I meant *now*."

Pete tossed a gold coin onto the bar and left. He rubbed his skinned knuckles as he walked to the livery where he had boarded Poseidon. Andy Dunson had that coming, he told himself, but he couldn't quite convince himself of that. It wasn't Dunson he despised; it was Cal Maddox, the hero of Dodge City, Kansas.

At the bank, Hannah smiled as Pete stuffed a collection of banknotes, checks, and coin into her satchel and handed it to her. Pete and Buddy followed her to the boardwalk, where a crowd—and Cal Maddox—had gathered. Trailed by Pecos and Pete, as well as a legion of admirers, she felt embarrassed at the cheers as Cal escorted her to the depot. The mayor and the editor of the *Times* had arranged for this, and a photographer asked them to stop underneath the wooden sign carved like a Winchester that advertised Zimmermann's hardware-tinware-gun store. The flash exploded, and someone handed her a bouquet of roses. She thought of Pete and his unfortunate trip to Fort Griffin. Cal Maddox was presented with cigars and whiskeys and a couple of kisses. Exhausted, Hannah rested on the bench outside the depot and waited to board the train. Pete carried her flowers and the satchel onto the passenger car.

"Mr. Maddox?" a reporter asked. "Time for a few final questions, sir?"

Cal nodded, excused himself, and disappeared around the platform.

"The queen prepares to leave as a crowd cheereth. The sun warms my face. Alas, why does my heart tremble so?"

Hannah smiled at J. W. Dougherty, resplendent in his new suit of black gabardine, double-breasted vest trimmed with red ribbon, and a wine-striped tie. Gray bowler at his side, he lifted her hand and kissed it gently.

"And what play is that from?" she asked.

"Actually, I made that one up." J. W.'s smile faded. "I've come to say good-bye, Hannah."

Hannah nodded sadly. Winter Wind had taken his fourteen dollars and ridden back to the Indian Territory right after the fire. The Mendiettas and Cadwallader had already gone, driving the rest of the remuda south to the Springer Ranch where they would pick up Chris and come home. Andy Dunson had disappeared without any good-byes, Irwin Sawyer had hired on with a crew driving breeding stock to the Dakotas, and Chito Ruthven had married a dance-hall girl and was trying a new life as a store clerk. The girl was still dancing.

So Hannah figured J. W. Dougherty would also go. Pete had bought train tickets home for himself, her, and Buddy Pecos. Cal Maddox purchased his own ticket, and the four of them were returning to Texas this afternoon on a big 4-6-0 Atchison, Topeka & Santa Fe locomotive heading east to Kansas City, Missouri. There they would catch another train to Denison, then one to Dallas, another to Waco, Austin, and San Antonio and finally on to Marfa, where they'd depart the rails and rent a buckboard to Fort Davis and home. Hannah was excited. She'd never ridden on a train. Pete seemed nervous. He had ridden trains but didn't like them. He didn't like anything that moved except horses. But she was sad to say farewell to J. W. Dougherty "What will you do?" she asked.

He smiled mischievously and withdrew a rolled-up newspaper from his back pocket. "There's an advertisement in the Caldwell *Journal* that the Corbett, James, and McHenry Troupe is performing *Antony and Cleopatra* at the Opera House next week. I'd like to see that tragedy and perhaps pay my respects backstage . . . if it is indeed the Corbett and James that I remember. I wonder who this McHenry is and whatever happened to Bobby Wilde and Jessie Larson. I shall find out."

"Be careful, Mr. Dougherty."

He smiled. " 'Heat not a furnace for your foe so hot that it do singe yourself.' Don't worry, Hannah. Take care of yourself." He stopped on the steps and turned around. His smile was gone. "Hannah," he said. A buggy passed. The train whistle blew. He studied his new boots, sighed, and stared at her. "I must tell you something that you probably do not desire to hear."

Hannah waited. Another lecture? Poetry or one final Shakespearean monologue?

"Cal Maddox set that fire in your hotel," Dougherty said.

Hannah sat dumbfounded. Dougherty wasn't joking. Her lips trembled, trying to choose words, a denial, something, but nothing came.

"You said two fires were burning when you stepped out of your room, one at the front stairway and another at the end of the hall, blocking you in," the cook continued. "That doesn't sound like an accident to me."

"Why would he do that?" she asked.

"To save you. To make an impression. To be a hero. To make you fall in love with him. I don't know. And I can't prove it," Dougherty said, pulling his derby low on his head. "But I know it. So does Pete."

"Why doesn't Pete—"

"Because Pete Belissari is nicer than I am. He doesn't want to hurt you, and, like me, he has no proof. I'm sorry, Hannah, but I thought you should know."

She listened as J. W. Dougherty hurried away, hearing laughter and muddled voices as Cal Maddox gave his last interview. Hannah bit her lip. Dougherty was wrong. Pete was wrong. They had to be. She was suddenly aware of a man's hand on her shoulder. She looked up.

"You ready to get on board?" Maddox asked.

She stared out the window, watching the rolling plains pass as the car rocked and the wheels clicked rhythmically. The Pullman had few passengers. Hannah sat alone, stretched out with her feet propped up on the opposite seat, her money satchel at her side. Across the aisle, Buddy Pecos played cards with Cal Maddox, while in front of her, Pete read from a book of Socrates he had found at Wright's store. Several rows ahead, a woman bounced an infant on her knee, a preacher read his Bible, and three men discussed Kansas politics.

The conductor walked past them, spinning his watch chain absently.

"Where we at, friend?" Maddox asked.

"Due west of Spearville. Next stop is Kinsley," the conductor answered and stepped outside.

Hannah glanced at Maddox and looked away. She closed her eyes, telling herself again that J. W. Dougherty had been wrong. The fire was an accident. Cal had happened along. He would never have risked her life just to make an impression.

"What the Sam Hill is he doin' here?" Pecos said.

She looked up. Andy Dunson weaved down the aisle, wearing a linen duster and new hat. His face looked awful, his nose swollen and disfigured, as if someone had plowed over him with a hay rake. He stopped, steadied himself with his left hand on the seat in front of Belissari, and said, "Howdy, folks." His breath smelled of strong whiskey.

Hannah blinked. When her eyes flashed open, Dunson had pulled a shotgun from underneath his duster and thumbed back both hammers, shoving the ugly barrels underneath Pete's nose.

"I'll take that bag of money," he told Hannah, though his eyes never left Pete. "Now!"

No one moved. The baby started crying, and one of the passengers up front started to rise. Dunson heard him. "Keep your seats, gents, or I spray these walls with Pete Belissari's brains."

The man sat down. Pete's revolver was stored unloaded in a canvas bag in the seat behind Hannah. Pecos and Maddox still wore their sidearms, but neither made a move. Hannah was glad. There was nothing anyone could do while Dunson held that shotgun in Pete's face.

"The money, lady. Now!" Dunson swore angrily, and shoved the shotgun against Pete's mustache.

"Don't," Hannah pleaded, and stood up, hefting the heavy satchel. She moved slowly. Dunson's eyes left Belissari and locked on her, though his shotgun didn't budge. He grinned as Hannah placed the bag at his worn boots and she backed away and sat down, holding her breath.

The cowhand squatted for the bag, and Pete moved. Hannah screamed.

Belissari had knocked the shotgun aside, trying to rise, but the passenger car lurched suddenly, and Pete fell off balance back into his seat. Dunson swore and brought the shotgun back into position. "No!" a voice shouted, and the shotgun roared.

Hannah gagged at the smell of acrid smoke. Her ears rang, and the voices sounded far away. The baby up front wailed. So did the mother. Hannah sprang to her feet, fanning away the terrible smoke, saw the window that had been blown apart by the shotgun blast, and thanked God when Pete slowly pulled himself to his feet. Andy Dunson sprawled on the floor, smoking shotgun at his fingers, and Cal Maddox towered over him, still holding his Colt. Blood oozed from Dunson's forehead, and the cowhand groaned. Cal must have jumped up and slammed his pistol barrel across Andy's forehead. She thanked God again.

Maddox swallowed and knelt by Dunson. Pecos holstered his own revolver, took off his hat, and ran his fingers through his thinning hair. "That was close," he said.

Pete started for the aisle when suddenly Cal swung the revolver in his direction and eared back the .45's hammer.

"Sit down!" Maddox said.

Chapter Nineteen

"Cal?" Hannah stared at him numbly, confused by his wild eyes as he reached for the satchel full of money.

Footsteps raced behind him, and Maddox spun around, snapping a shot at a rushing passenger. Blood rained on a window as the man grasped his left shoulder and pitched into the seat, moaning. Maddox stumbled backward and aimed the Colt first at Pecos, then at Pete. Neither moved. Mother and child sobbed and sank to the floor, the preacher closed his eyes and silently prayed, and the two other passengers sat timidly in their seats and raised their hands.

"Cal," Hannah pleaded. "Don't."

Maddox licked his lips and pulled himself up, satchel in his left hand, smoking Colt in his right. He considered Andy Dunson briefly, glanced over his shoulder, and stared at Hannah.

"Come with me," he told her.

Hannah couldn't think. Maybe she shook her head. She couldn't tell, but she must have done something because Cal pleaded with her now. "Come on, Hannah. There's more'n seventy thousand dollars here. Do you know how far that can take us?"

Her stomach turned. She forced herself to swallow despite a parched throat. "Cal," she finally said, "you're not thinking."

He laughed, though without humor. "I told you I never thought things through, but this is our chance, Hannah. A new life. But we gotta hurry."

"No." She almost shouted this.

Maddox's eyes hardened. "What do you want?" he flared and swore. "To go back to that hardscrabble ranch and them kids that ain't even yours? This is seventy-five thousand dollars! *Ours!*"

"You can't get away," Pecos said flatly.

Cal checked around him and studied the door briefly. "Hannah, Dunson has two horses waitin' right outside Spearville. We can use them. Please."

Hannah trembled. "How do you know that?" she asked.

Cal didn't reply. The wounded man moaned. The preacher now cited the Lord's Prayer audibly. Maddox didn't have to answer. She knew, or could guess. Andy Dunson had helped Cal set the fire at the Bisland. In turn, Cal promised to help Dunson in this robbery if something went wrong, for a split. Only Cal saw a better chance when he . . .

She shook her head.

The conductor barged through the door. "What in the name of—" Maddox lunged at him, buried the butt of his revolver into the man's forehead, and shoved him into Buddy Pecos's lap, then ran, slamming the door behind him. The glass in the door shattered. For a second, she thought the force had smashed the window before realizing Cal had fired his Colt again, a warning shot. Everyone ducked behind the seats for what seemed like minutes.

Hannah felt paralyzed. Not Pete. He was up in a second, pulling a short-barreled Colt from Dunson's holster and bolting out the door after Maddox and the money.

Pecos also moved, shoving the unconscious conductor aside and ordering the two politics-talking passengers to see to the wounded men. "Stay here," he told Hannah and put his hand on the doorknob.

"Hold it, Pecos!" Dunson slurred his words, and slowly pulled himself up to a seated position on the floor. He held the shotgun loosely in his arms. Pecos turned around, releasing his grip. Dunson grimaced and tried to rise but couldn't.

"We'll wait a spell," Dunson said. "Till I can walk." He motioned with the shotgun. "I still got one barrel left, and I'll blow the first body to move to oblivion." His eyes searched the floor. "Where's Maddox?"

"He took the money," Pecos answered.

"That double-crossin' son of . . ."

Pete paused on the platform and looked around. Maddox hadn't jumped off the train, had he? He surely hadn't gone into the adjoining Pullman. He heard the clicking of the wheels, as the train swayed. Something sounded on the roof of the next car. Pete shoved the Colt into his waistband and leaned against the secured ladder, grabbing the nearest rungs. He pulled himself up and looked down at the ground speeding past him.

Don't do that again, he told himself, trying to block out all of the newspaper stories he had read about brakemen being crushed to death trying to work the link-and-pin couplers that connected the cars. He looked skyward and pulled himself up, one step at a time, then cautiously peered over the top of the roof. Maddox ran toward the front of the train, somehow balancing himself despite the pitching motion. With a groan, Belissari gripped the hand brake on the top of the Pullman and climbed onto the roof.

He stood up. He knelt down. Sweat dampened his face and shirt, and he sucked in a lungful of thick, black smoke. The train swayed, and the smoke changed directions. Pete wiped his eyes and rose, gingerly moving across the roof as the wind whipped his face. His left moccasin slipped, and Pete fell to his hands and knees, breathing rapidly, heart pounding.

"Did I ever tell you how I hopped trains in Kansas and Chicago?"

Pete cringed. Cal Maddox smiled down at him.

"All of the time," Maddox answered his own question. "This is as easy as ridin' a horse for me."

The smile vanished. Maddox brought his right leg up and slammed his boot under Pete's chin.

Pete collapsed and felt himself sliding off the roof. He clawed frantically for a grip, smelling cinder-thick smoke and death. He went over the side, but somehow managed to bury his fingers on the edge of the roof. His feet slammed against the side of the Pullman. Pete looked into a window and glimpsed a horrible face staring at him, eyes wide with fear. It took a moment to realize it was his reflection.

He looked down again. Kansas sped below him. The clicking of the wheels sounded menacing now, not soothing. He tried to pull himself up, made it halfway, but Maddox shoved him again.

No *ta'ma* came to Belissari. There was no time to pray. He stared into Cal's eyes. The cowboy squatted beside him as Belissari swayed and squirmed and tried to hold on.

"I figured you'd come after me," Maddox said before making sure no one else had climbed on the roof. "I should shoot you, but this'll do fine."

Where is Buddy? Pete's brain screamed.

Maddox's hat sailed away in a gust of wind that carried another fog of smoke over them. Belissari's eyes burned. Soot covered Cal's face, giving him the appearance of some battle-hardened Trojan warrior sworn to revenge.

Maddox coughed. "We're almost to Spearville," he said. "Time for me to disembark. And you too. When you fall, push yourself away from the tracks. Else you might get caught under the wheels, and that can be . . . well . . . bloody. I do hope you only break some bones. Murder don't set right with me."

Maddox slammed the satchel against Pete's right hand. Belissari yelled as he lost his grip. He swallowed, straining to hold on with his left hand. Maddox leaned over and laughed. Pete's right hand brushed across his body, pressed against the window for a second and jerked the Colt from his waistband. Cal's eyes widened. Gasping, he tried to move away. Not fast enough. Pete drove the Colt's walnut butt down on Maddox's fingers.

A piercing scream sounded as Maddox spun and tumbled away from Belissari across the roof. Pete dropped the .45, swore softly, and put his right hand on top of the car. He strained, groaned, his moccasins slipping and sliding against the window. He dropped again, pulled himself up, and slammed his right foot through the glass.

A spearlike shard tore through the leather and into his foot. Another ripped his calf. Blood soaked his moccasin, but he had a good perch now. He looked up, saw the satchel but no Cal Maddox, and wrestled his way to the top of the car, pulling his bloody foot free, ignoring the pain. Air, fresh air, filled his lungs. He saw Cal Maddox hanging over the side, struggling. Pete moved, limping, but his right leg buckled, and he fell facedown on the roof. Breathing heavily, Pete rolled over on hands and knees. He reached for the satchel, but Maddox grabbed it first. The cowboy kicked at Pete's face, missed, and raced across the roof. Maddox leaped onto the next car, but this time the train careened and sent Cal sprawling, hanging on to the car's smokestack. Pete followed, hobbling, bouncing to keep his balance, and jumped from roof to roof. He slipped again, kissing the top of the car. Maddox struggled to his feet. Pete reared back and kicked, sending Maddox skating toward the edge. The smoke now was choking, thick and black, and he smelled burning wood. They had to be near the locomotive. Pete grabbed for the satchel, caught a glimpse of Maddox's fist, and tried to duck. He rolled with the punch, skidded across the roof. He couldn't breathe but had to move, get up. His foot felt raw. Belissari turned. Cal Maddox buried his shoulder into Pete's stomach. Pete felt himself flying now, filled his lungs with smoke again, and landed hard, painfully. Breathing hurt. He tasted blood and knew he had broken a few ribs.

He weaved, rolled over, gripping chunks of wood and filling his left palm with splinters, feeling blood flow down his left side. He realized they had landed in the long tender behind the locomotive. Maddox groaned, spit out a tooth, swore angrily. Belissari's eyes burned. He tried to rub them quickly. Mistake! He saw Cal moving, reacted. Pete ducked as a piece of wood sailed past his ear. The two men stumbled to unsteady standing positions, locking their arms, trying to balance their feet on the woodpile, swearing at each other between grunts.

And then they were flying again, as metal screeched against metal, steam hissed, and they slammed violently into solid ground.

Andy Dunson pulled himself to his feet. A crowd had gathered at both ends of the Pullman from the neighboring cars. He hesitated, licking his lips.

"Give it up," Pecos told him. "You got nowheres to go."

Dunson pointed the scattergun at Hannah. "We're goin' together," he told her. "We're jumpin' off at Spearville and gettin' out of here." He stared hard at Pecos. "You try to stop me, and I'll blow her head off. Ease that six-gun with your left hand and hand it to me, butt forward."

Hannah saw the hatred in Pecos's cold eye, but the gunman did as he was commanded. Dunson shoved the Schofield in his empty holster and snapped at Hannah. "Get up!" He swung the shotgun at Buddy's midriff. "And you sit down!"

She rose, slowly. Dunson stared at Pecos as the tall Texan eased his lanky frame into the nearest seat. *Think!* Hannah told herself. Do something. She saw the cord above the window, reached quickly, and yanked it hard.

"What the—" Dunson began, but the train's brakes screamed. Hannah pitched forward, flipped over the seat, landing hard, jamming her shoulder against the floor. She was vaguely aware that all motion had stopped, heard some dreadful noise and pulled herself to her feet. Buddy Pecos straddled Andy Dunson, mercilessly pounding the cowboy's already mangled face.

"Pete!" Hannah said, shoved through the crowd and onto the platform, leaped to the ground, looked west and east. She saw the two men rising from the tallgrass and ran toward the coughing locomotive.

She stopped, stared. Pete limped slowly, trying to land a good grip on the ripped front of Maddox's shirt. Hannah gasped at the bloody figures. The two men lunged at each other. Pete blocked one punch, but Maddox sent his right fist into Belissari's stomach. Pete doubled over. Hannah was running now, screaming for Cal to stop. Instead, Maddox grabbed Pete's shirttail and slammed his head against the side of the tender. Belissari crumpled near the rails, and, heaving, Maddox drew his Colt, thumbed back the hammer.

"No!" Hannah screamed.

Maddox spun around, finally hearing her. The barrel swung in her direction.

"Cal," she said. "It's over."

Passengers poured out of the Pullmans, some of them brandishing weapons, pointing at the reckless-eyed cowboy. Maddox turned, but the engineer, wielding a giant wrench, and two other men blocked his path. Two hundred yards away, maybe less, two hobbled horses grazed nonchalantly. Spearville! Maddox spun around and sprinted to Hannah. She tried to turn and run, but he caught her and pulled her close, his left arm crushing her stomach. The Colt's cold barrel pushed up her chin.

"Nobody!" Cal yelled. "Nobody moves or I kill her!" He added with a whisper, "Sorry, honey, but I'm all out of choices. Reckon this'll have to be our dance. See them horses? We're ridin' out."

They moved only a few steps before Maddox straightened. "You!" he yelled.

The engineer lowered the wrench. "Find that satchel and bring it here. I ain't leavin' without that money."

Dumbfounded, the man shook his burly head. "What satchel?"

Cal started to reply, aimed the Colt at the engineer. Hannah saw a chance and slammed both heels on Maddox's toes. The cowboy yelled. Hannah felt herself jerked to the ground. A gunshot exploded. She rolled over, sat up, and found Cal Maddox spreadeagle on the ground, blood cascading from his nose and mouth. Pete hovered over him, wobbly, and dropped a piece of firewood on the ground by the unconscious cowboy. He stared down at the Maddox's prostrate form, and despite his bloody foot, drew back and buried a moccasin in Cal's side. Even a sudden blast of steam from the locomotive didn't drown out Belissari's burst of profanity.

Chapter Twenty

Sitting in the sleeper car, Pete ground his teeth as Buddy Pecos wrapped the torn sheets around the broken ribs and stitches. The sharpshooter had already put fresh bandages on Pete's other wounds and helped him into his boots. Pecos tied the muslin and stepped back. "Hold your arms out like you're an eagle," Pecos ordered. Pete did as he was told, closing his eyes against the pain.

"Hurt when you do that?" Pecos asked.

"Yes."

"Then don't do that."

Smiling, Belissari shook his head and painfully pulled on his shirt. "You're about as good of a doctor as you are a humorist," Pete told him.

"Humor what?"

"Never mind."

Pete rose with help from the cane a passenger had given him in Kansas City and looked down at the stovepipe boots he had been forced to buy in Kinsley. They were two different sizes, the larger one for his heavily bandaged right foot. "Those boots ain't gonna do you no good once you're all healed," Pecos had told him. "I don't intend to wear them after that," Pete had answered.

"Well," Pecos said now. "We're almost home. I'm thinkin' 'bout having a whiskey in the dinin' room. Care to join me?"

Pete shook his head. "Maybe later," he said, and limped out of the Pullman sleeper and into the passenger cars. He glanced out the window as he hobbled down the aisle. Beautiful West Texas sped past him. They had just pulled out of Marathon. Next stop, Marfa. Home. He should be smiling.

He slid into the seat across Hannah. She twiddled her thumbs, stared at her feet, things she never did. Belissari tried to think of something to say, couldn't. He thought about Kinsley, where they had left Cal Maddox and Andy Dunson in jail and where a doctor had patched up Pete's wounds.

"That's all I can do for you, son," Pete remembered the old sawbones saying.

"And what can you do for her?" he asked, nodding in Hannah's direction.

The doctor had cleared his throat, answering softly, "That's your department, your patient. Good luck."

Hannah had hardly spoken since the attempted robbery. The satchel of money stayed at her side, but Pete doubted if she would notice if anyone came by and took it. Maybe she wouldn't even care.

He cleared his throat. She didn't look up. He talked anyway. "So Buddy's putting on a new bandage," he said, "and he tells me to stretch my arms out like an eagle. I do. Hurts like tarnation. He says, 'Does it hurt when you do that?' 'Yeah,' I tell him. And Buddy says, 'Well, don't do that.' " Pete laughed. Hannah didn't.

With a sigh, Pete ran his fingers through his hair. "Guess it was funnier then," he said softly.

Hannah looked up at him. She didn't say anything, just stared back with those melancholy blue eyes.

He closed his eyes, and they rode on in silence. The whistle screamed out a series of short toots. Pete tried to think. He'd been on trains long enough now that he should understand the signals. He looked out the window and smiled, not even noticing the other whistles. The train began to slow. Steam hissed, and the brakes squealed. He tapped on the window and said, "Hannah . . ."

She looked up. People milled about the Pullman, grabbing their bags. Hannah peeked out the window. Pete laughed as she leaped to her feet and ran to the outside platform, probably jumping to the depot before the train had completely stopped. He struggled to rise, grabbed the satchel, and fell in line.

"Have a nice day," the conductor told him.

Pete saw her then, sitting in the middle of Marfa

Station, hugging and kissing Cynthia and Angelica and Paco and Bruce and Desmond and Darcy. She even let the dog lick her face, and Hannah had never cared much for that dog. People passed them, smiling. Belissari tried to savor the moment as he leaned against a lamppost, watched, listened, almost laughed himself.

"Tell us all about it, Mama Hannah!"

"When will Chris get home?"

"Did you see any Injuns?"

"Where's Pete and Buddy?"

"What did you bring us? What did you bring us?"

"Can I go on a cattle drive next year?"

"Desmond has a centipede for a pet in a jar, but I don't like it."

"Darcy broke my dolly, Mama Hannah."

"I don't like that new schoolteacher. He don't teach nothing like you do."

Hannah laughed so hard she clutched her side.

"You know, Pete, you might be a miracle worker." Pete looked at Buddy Pecos. The gunman smiled, patted Pete's back, and drifted away. Pete pulled on his hat, his smile fading, feeling bittersweet.

"Not quite," he said softly.

He felt better, but this wasn't what he needed, really. Slowly Pete started to walk away, to gather their luggage and rent a buckboard for the trip to Fort Davis. "Pete!" Paco screamed. Pete turned, dropping cane and satchel. "Paco," Pete told the running boy, speeding up his plea: "Paco, don't-jump-on-me-I've-got-brok—"

Man and boy crashed to the hardwood floor.

Barefoot, hatless, wearing only his trousers and summer undershirt, Belissari sat on the side of his bunk in the shed off the barn. He slowly pulled the long needle and string of sinew through the piece of deerskin, examined his handiwork, and continued. The long, waxy thread made from a deer's tendon had needles attached on both ends. Pete pulled the other needle through the hole in the leather he had made with an awl. The sinew tightened.

"May I come in?"

He looked up, saw Hannah in a plain green dress, and nodded. Pete continued sewing his new pair of moccasins. Hannah sat beside him, staring as he concentrated on his work. She smelled of flour. She smelled wonderful.

"You're pretty good at that," she said softly.

"It's called saddle stitching," he explained. "Good for leather work. I had plenty of practice before . . ." He had started to say "before I met you." He tossed the unfinished footwear on his pillow, wished he had shaved this morning.

"How are you?" he asked.

Hannah cleared her throat. "I . . . I thought . . . I thought we could talk some."

"I'd like that."

They fell silent. The wind picked up outside. Maybe it would rain. Pete doubted it.

Hannah was shaking. Pete started to put his arm around her, stopped, uncertain, then did it anyway. She rested her head against his shoulder. Hannah sobbed quietly. "It's all right," he whispered to her.

She pulled away, looked into his eyes. "Pete . . . I'm . . . I'm sorry."

Tears spilled from her blue eyes as she cried harder. "I . . . I . . . I . . ."

"Shhhhh," he said, and pulled her closer. "It's all right."

"No, it's not. I treated you . . . I got . . . I . . . I was wrong."

"No," he said firmly and pushed her gently away from her so he could look her into her eyes. "I was wrong, Hannah. I would have left those cattle here, to die. You got them to Kansas. You did that. Not me. Not Buddy. Not Julian Cale. You saved this place and every rancher who sent cattle with us."

Hannah wiped her nose and eyes. "For what?" she blurted out. "I got Paul Richmond killed, almost killed Mr. Cale."

"Those were accidents, Hannah," he argued. "They could have happened anywhere, to anyone, any time. No one's to blame. And if you hadn't pushed on, made us keep going, this ranch wouldn't be ours, yours."

She bowed her head, sobbed more. "Yeah, all I did was buy us another year."

Pete laughed softly and pulled her to him. "That's the best anybody can hope for in these parts, Hannah," he told her. "You know that better than anyone." She buried her face into his shirt, wrapped her arms around him, and squeezed, forgetting about his broken ribs and

stitches, crying harder now. "But . . . but . . . it . . . was
. . . so hard."

He rocked her on the bed, kissed her hair, let the
sorrow run its course. "It's all right," he said. "It's
going to be all right." She needed to cry. She had held
back for too long, steeled herself, but now it was over.
He knew she was crying for Dardanus and El Moro
and all of the other animals that had died on the drive,
for Julian Cale and especially poor Paul Richmond, for
Chris, himself, probably even for Cal Maddox. That
was all right, too. Pete didn't hate Cal anymore.

Pete rested his left hand against the small of her
back. He caught the scent of rain in the wind. Could
it be? It didn't matter. If it rained today or tomorrow,
there would be other obstacles, other droughts, flash
floods and blizzards, low prices for cattle and high expenses. That was the game of ranching in West Texas.
The weather didn't matter. He kissed Hannah again.
This was all that mattered.

"I love you," he told her.

"I love you too," she said between sobs. "Don't
leave me."

"I won't," he said. Pete had no plans of ever leaving
Hannah Scott. He was here for her. He always had
been, always would be, now, tomorrow, for as long as
he breathed.